A

Sudden

Emotional

Chaos

by Yomi Akinode

Printed in the United States of America

First Printing: May 2024

Paperback

B0D3B3N721

Table of Contents

Chapter 1

Father Joe Fantone had dedicated his life to serving others. His recurring work challenges were to encourage and help unfortunate souls who had lost their way.

His favorite prodigal embodiment was Billy Pearse, a solitary man who rose from the abyss. He felt privileged to tell his family story.

The source of Billy's detached behavior from age seventeen had long been a sore point for his parents, long before his father died, leaving his mother and four kids to fend for themselves.

In the summer of 1983, Florence Pearse moved her children, Billy, her firstborn, twenty-four, and his siblings, Kyle, fourteen, Sylvia, nine, and Jordan, five, from rural Georgia to San Diego when their father died.

They stayed with Aunt Mona, Florence's twin sister.

Aunt Mona was a successful actress who, a year later, died filming a movie scene at Trocadero, leaving Florence with only one other distant living relative, Nana Bertha, down in Georgia.

The insurance payment from Aunt Mona held Florence and her brood over until it ran out, and she became a multi-janitorial worker in the ubiquitous manufacturing facilities that dotted the Southern California Mediterranean climatic abeyance.

Ten years to the day after the El Cajon relocation, the Florence Pearse household was on the verge of the family's first college graduate: the eldest, Billy Pearse.

She patiently waited at home for Billy to return with his graduation gown and cap.

After the joyous occasion, she left for her janitorial work.

Throughout her ordeal, as the kids grew, Florence's sole focus was clearly on their education. She aspired for all of them to graduate from college.

Years earlier, Billy eavesdropped upon an argument with his mother's twin sister before she passed...

"Acting isn't a job, Flo... " It's an avenue for fat, grubby men to paw all over my beautiful behind," Aunt Mona said as she strutted in her bikini, getting her wardrobe ready for another shoot. But then, she turned to face Florence's accusatory demeanor in all seriousness.

"What would you have me do, Flo? We were both orphaned early and without any meaningful education..."

She walked off before turning to face Florence sharply again.

"Promise me your kids will get the best education possible."

Florence tried to gloss over the promise, but Aunt Mona would have none. She insisted. “Promise me, Flo.”

Billy’s mother relented and promised, then caught Billy listening by the door. She coyly pulled off her slippers and threw them at the door, barely missing him as he ran off.

A decade later, the promise of education was on the verge of its first fulfillment.

***

It was getting darker outside in April 1983.

Billy’s hand was held tight onto the plastic bag as he shimmied himself amongst the crowd for a better position at a glass window outside an electronics store in El Cajon, a town east of San Diego.

Their noses pressed against the window, and they watched the space shuttle Challenger’s maiden flight launch with rapt attention. His vision veered to the store wall clock. “Oh, Shaiza,” escaped his mouth. His mother warned them not to swear.

He was immediately bullied out of the cheering crowd and ran fast down the street.

He was breathing hard when he entered the apartment complex and ran across the parking lot to the building’s front door.

Inside, he flew up the staircase with excitement and busted into their third-floor apartment two steps at a time.

In her green janitorial work uniform, his mother, Florence Pearse, rushed towards him; Kyle, his younger brother; Sylvia, his younger sister; and Jordan, the youngest, were not far behind.

His mother stopped, and they all ran into her from behind like a brick wall. She was too excited to notice as she stared Billy down, pointing at the bag in his hand.

"It ain't gonna show itself in them cellophane bag, boy!"

Billy stopped at the center table and pulled out his graduation gown and cap from the plastic bag.

Kyle immediately snatched the cap and ran off with it on his head. Billy reared angrily; his mother calmed him with a look and inspected the gown as if it were a delicate ornament.

She glanced up with her arms spread out wide to all her children, and in a husky voice, she called out, "Group huuuug," and then quickly wiped away her tears before anyone saw it as the embrace ended.

Kyle returned the cap and planted himself in front of Billy. "What does an Industrial Engineer do anyway?"

He ruffled his hair. "You ever feel angry when you stand too long in the grocery line checkouts? Or when Mama takes too long to cook dinner?"

"What?" Kyle asked, confused, then lost interest and walked away.

Sylvia sidled up to her mother. "You working today, Mama?"

Her mother unlocked the balcony door, stepped out, and picked up one of the four empty apple boxes for grocery shopping that were lying against the wall.

She stepped back inside, dropped the box, turned, closed the glass sliding door behind her, locked it, and double-checked the lock.

Now ready to leave for work, Jordan, the five-year-old, tied himself to her leg, and they both dragged themselves towards the front door. Billy's mother turned by the door, looking at Billy. "I'm working late tonight; keep an eye on your brothers and sisters."

She peeled Jordan off her leg, kissed his smiling face, picked up the apple box, and walked out the door.

***

Billy's best friend walked in an hour after his mother left. They shook hands, and he flopped on the sofa beside Billy while Kyle, Sylvia, and Jordan played in the lounge near them.

Billy walked off and soon returned with a bottle of beer.

He threw a bottle at his friend and turned up the record player.

Kyle wasn't too thrilled about the noise. "Hey, come on, man!"

Billy interrupted him firmly with a command. "Bedroom now with all of ya; I need the space."

"I'm telling Mama," Kyle threatened, but rounded up Sylvia, reading at a corner, and Jordan, pushing a plastic car.

Kyle played in the bedroom with an R2-D2 toy and a plastic lightsaber.

Sylvia read on the bed, a Cabbage Patch Kid doll on her chest.

While Jordan looked lost, Kyle threw one of his toy cars at him.

Jordan stood in the middle of the room, twiddling with the car.

In the lounge, Billy and his friend drunk-slept, snoring.

When it was dark outside, the friend groaned, staggered towards the balcony, knocked empty beer bottles off the center table, unlocked the sliding door, and stepped out onto the balcony.

He shoved apple boxes off with his foot and made room at the railing, resting his arms as he stared down below at the well-lit and busy parking lot.

He inhaled deeply, shuddered, and returned inside, leaving the sliding door half-open.

He flopped back on the sofa next to an unconscious Billy and fell asleep again.

The bedroom door opened. Jordan walked out with his toy car and tugged Billy's pants, which didn't move. He turned to Billy's friend and watched him snore with his mouth open, drool slipping out. Then a loud car horn blast caught Jordan, the five-year-old's attention; he turned toward the sound and walked to the balcony.

He dropped his car toy, play-pushed the apple boxes, and soon pushed the boxes flush to the railing.

He climbed atop the box. Right then, his mother walked through the parking lot with groceries.

With her apartment balcony in full view, she saw an object fall from it and splatter onto the asphalt. She dropped everything and ran towards the object.

It was Jordan who had hit the ground.

She screamed, clutched at her heart, collapsed, and died of a heart attack next to her youngest son. She was forty years old.

The morbid event was exacerbated when all the children flew to the parking lot.

Unfortunately, they witnessed the macabre display of human tragedy, laid bare on the asphalt, before the emergency and law enforcement agencies arrived.

The tragedy's repercussions would manifest significantly in all of their future endeavors.

Chapter 2

Once the cops arrived at the scene, they immediately removed the kids as far away as possible from the gore. But they'd already been exposed for too long.

The parking lot was cleared late in the evening, and the coroner's vehicles left.

The local police Chief and a social services official returned the children to the apartment.

The mood was predictably sour as the Chief gently asked, "Is there anyone you can call to stay with you overnight?"

"Yes, sir. Aunt Mona," Billy answered.

"But..." Sylvia began to say. Kyle, beside her on the sofa, pinched her to stop.

The Chief caught on. "Young lady? You wanted to say?"

Sylvia dropped her gaze and said nothing. She then looked up. "May I go to the bathroom, please?" She left the room.

The Chief asked, "Why is your Aunt not here now?"

"What?" Billy asked.

“Your Aunt? I cannot leave you alone without adult supervision. I have kids the same age as you, and I cannot imagine the trauma. Is there anyone else to call?”

“Oh, she was in LA at a shoot when I called her. She’s driving back now,” Billy answered.

“Shoot?”

“She’s an actress.”

The Chief stood up, paced the lounge, and looked at the social services official who took over.

“How are you kids set up for food? You’re certainly not going to be left here alone tonight. If necessary, I’ll take all of you home with me.”

Bill jumped in. “We’re fine. Mama always had food,” and Sylvia began to cry again. Kyle led her off the couch and walked towards the bedroom.

“I cannot leave you here alone,” the worried Chief insisted.

“Can people come for us in the morning to work out the next steps?” Billy suggested, void of emotion, surprising the Chief.

“How old are you, son?” The Chief asked.

Billy was reticent. “Twenty-four.”

“That’s old enough, son, but this is much heavier than you think once it starts to sink in. Please, let me help you.

You cannot stay alone with your siblings, at least not tonight."

Billy sighed, knowing the Chief was right but afraid of being split from Kyle and Sylvia. Mama had warned them multiple times, simulating just what was happening now.

"Would you like to bring your brother and sister to my place tonight if social services do not have immediate accommodation?" The Chief suggested.

Billy thought it over some more and made a suggestion. "Can the social services officer stay with us here tonight? I don't want us to sleep in a strange place."

The Chief looked at him and reluctantly agreed.

"I need to complete some paperwork at the office. I'll be gone for less than thirty minutes and return. Meanwhile, the social services officer will remain behind while I'm gone."

The social services officer nodded his agreement.

"Thank you, Sir," Billy replied.

***

Florence had drilled into her kids' memories that they were each other's best resource for survival the moment their father had walked out years earlier.

Billy sat them down in the lounge as they packed boxes and talked to them.

"You remember what Mama always said?"

Sylvia rubbed the sleep from her eyes.

"Yes. We're our sister's keepers," Kyle said lazily, yawning.

"Her exact words at the time were… 'if anything happens to me, Nana Bertha will always have a home for you.'" Billy added.

"Are we going to Georgia?" Sylvia asked.

"Yes."

Fifteen minutes after the Chief left and the social services officer went out for a smoke, Billy took his siblings and boarded a Greyhound bus for Georgia.

***

In a wheelchair, Nana Bertha welcomed them to her small ranch, overgrown with weeds.

As expected, eighty-four-year-old Nana Bertha had a home filled with souvenirs and a notable standout collection of fabric dolls that occupied a measurable section of her lounge.

"Your mama was very kind to me when my distant nephew, her husband, your father, was stealing my money and jewelry to stick up his nose." She demonstrated the act.

“Thank you for having us, Nana…” Billy began to say, but she interrupted.

“You lot were a godsend. I was about to hire some live-in nurse, as you can see…” she pointed to sections of the lounge covered in dust, “but I’m glad to help. Your mother was a good person.”

She looked at Sylvia, cozied up next to Kyle, and her eyes fixated on the bevy of dolls that challenged your psyche not to gaze.

“Those are my babies, child, quite valuable. I’ll never get rid of them for anything.”

She turned to Billy. “When are you coming back to live with us?”

“You’re leaving?” Kyle was stunned.

“I have to go back, or social services will come looking for us,” Billy said.

“Oh, but you’re coming back, right?”

“Soon. You only need to take care of Sylvia until then.” Billy added.

“Okay, then, children. Dinner ain’t going to make itself,” Nana stated flatly and then turned to Sylvia.

“At your age, Missy, I was already whipping a casserole for my Pa.”

Sylvia burst into tears and ran out of the room; Kyle followed her.

Billy stiffened. “Nana Bertha. Sylvia is very fragile; she will need your help without Mama, please.”

“Okay, Billy, but don’t take too long. I ain’t getting any younger.”

Billy left two days later and returned to San Diego.

He would not see either of his siblings for several years.

***

It’d been a hard ten years since the dastardly incident of his brother’s death fall, as he ruminated over bourbon at a bar in Old Town, San Diego.

Billy had always only blamed himself for Jordan’s death and, ultimately, their mother’s. He was in a constant state of shame, remorse, and sadness.

Billy always thought that the more isolated he was from his siblings, especially Kyle, the better it was for them. He rationalized that Kyle, being fourteen when the chaos occurred, had specific awareness of the horror, and Sylvia, only nine, still had time to recover.

It was late evening, and he and the bar patron were stunned agog at the First World Trade Center bombing chaos playing out on television. Drunk, he laid money on the bar and staggered out onto the street towards a homeless Tent City.

Billy Pearse, now thirty-four years old, wore his six-foot-two handsome bearing quite poorly due to poor living conditions and excessive alcohol consumption.

His gaunt, haggard face navigated a shortcut under the bridge, through the Tent City dirt road, when two black vans hemmed the road at either end of him. Plainclothes Cops jumped out and swept him and everyone on the road into vans.

He challenged the desk sergeant at the precinct, "What's the charge?"

"Your ugly face." The officer glared.

"You wearing your glasses, Serg?" Billy snickered.

The sergeant looked him over and chuckled sarcastically at his clothing. "You stink," he concluded.

Billy looked him over in anger. "Yeah? You're racist."

The sergeant turned to the bullpen behind him, yelled, and pointed at him. "Can someone take care of this bozo here?"

A uniformed officer came out from behind the counter and roughly dragged Billy away.

After an hour in detention, a white van behind the precinct drove them off to a nearby sanatorium, and the guards shoved them into rooms with roommates, oblivious to ceiling CCTV cameras.

The guards locked them in.

Billy went straight to bed and soon fell into a fitful, nightmarish sleep...

A loud car horn from the balcony caught Jordan's attention, and Billy, on the sofa, watched Jordan walk onto the balcony.

He saw Jordan climb atop the apple box. Billy walked off the sofa, leaned against the balcony sliding door jamb, and watched Jordan fall off the balcony.

He casually walked to the railing, stared below at the parking lot, and saw his mother screaming before she slumped down next to Jordan, dead.

Billy started to laugh hysterically.

Gasping, Billy awoke in a cold sweat at the sanatorium, whimpering.

Hours later, a guard pushed him into a white office and locked him in.

He sat, discomfited, on a straight-backed chair opposite a desk as a man in a black cassock walked in, smiling. Billy smirked in defiance.

As he came to learn his name, Father Joe Fantone leaned on the desk, looked him straight in the eye, and talked in a measured, pleasant tone. "San Diego Chamber of Commerce is not my favorite place to be, either. The chamber owns the sanatorium."

Billy remained quiet in confusion, staring malevolently at the cleric, who leaned in closer. "Why were you at Tent City?"

Billy answered without hesitation. "To drink."

"I'm Irish myself," Father Joe retorted.

"Breakfast of Champions" Was Billy's comeback.

Father Joe migrated to sit behind the desk.

"CCTV showed you in hysterics last night. Want to talk about it?"

"When can I get out of here?" Billy challenged.

The Holy man started to say, gesturing with a smile... "What worked for me in the past... You become selfless in pursuit of happiness, but not in this nut house."

Billy leaned forward. "Are you allowed to say 'nut house'?"

Father Joe pointed a finger at the heavens. "He doesn't mind. Do you?"

Billy didn't respond, so the Father continued. "You don't care much that you're incarcerated in a sanatorium?" Billy shrugged.

"You would have bailed yourself out yesterday if you wanted to. Do you have a family?" The cleric asked.

Billy tightened up. Father Joe noticed. "I hate to pry, but I can help. Need me to call anyone?"

"I'm tired, Father."

The papal smiled. "Free and no encumbrances, huh?"

Billy exploded in anger. "Ain't nothing free, I tell you."

Then, he took a deep breath, calmed down, and launched into a rant. "It's impossible to run away from yourself forever. Eventually, you catch up with yourself."

"Are you running from something, son?"

"Let me out of here, Father."

The clergy studied him more closely, to Billy's discomfort.

"Uhm. I'm guessing there's more to you, mister..." the cleric's voice trailed off.

They both fell into silence, staring each other down.

Billy perked up in anger. "You sit up there, so judgmental. What's your story, Father?"

The Father did not reply immediately. He walked to the wall and turned to face Billy, his back resting on the wall, arms folded.

"Of what good would my story be to you, son?"

Billy laughed mirthlessly. "It's what I thought. What's good for the goose is never good for the gander."

"So, you think I'm not genuine?" the Father asked. Billy shrugged.

The Father then returned to sit behind his desk. He leaned forward and signaled Billy to come closer.

"My father was an old Italian mobster from Genoa when he landed in America with a wife and two young kids. He became overwhelmed and strayed."

Father Joe Fantone stopped talking long enough for Billy to ask, "And?"

"He left my mother within two days of arrival and joined the gangs in New York, running numbers. My sister, who was autistic, was devastated and ended up in an asylum, not different from where we are now.

"I went to the priesthood and my sister, Isabella, to the Nunnery. My mother still lives in Poughkeepsie, upstate New York. Have I satisfied your curiosity?"

"And your sister?" Billy asked, confusing the cleric.

"My sister, what?"

Billy became recalcitrant. “Which Nunnery?”

Father Fantone’s eyebrows furrowed. “Why is that important, son?”

“It’s not. I’m making conversation.”

The office door opened, and a guard led Billy away.

Father Fantone spoke before the door closed. “Abbey of Saint Walburga, Virginia Dale, Colorado.”

Billy Pearse turned to look at the priest expressionlessly.

Chapter 3

Years later, Billy Pearse sat in his office as the Safety Engineer Manager for Zobo Pumps, a pump assembly factory in North Park, San Diego, with a half-empty salad bowl next to the soup cup on his desk as he finished reading the newspaper headline.

'Human genome mapping completed.'

"Ain't that somethin'," he mumbled.

He dropped the newspaper, and his cell phone rang as he adjusted the portrait of his girlfriend, Judy.

"Sylvia" popped up on the caller ID, and he ignored the call.

The voicemail message sounded pinged, so he retrieved the message.

"I'll never give up on you, as you've given up on us, Billy; I miss you something awful. Please call me..."

Each time Sylvia or Kyle called, Billy always found himself mentally dragged back to the death ordeals and felt the more he engaged with his siblings, the worse it'd be for them.

He was in a self-induced abject state when a loud emergency alarm went off in the factory. Billy cut off the voicemail, rushed out, and joined others as they spewed out of offices.

On the factory floor, a circle formed near the boom lift whose heavy chain links still dangled. A woman in a green janitorial uniform lay in a pool of blood on the floor under the boom lift. A large pump at the end of the boom chain rested inside her torso.

Next to her was a leaky mop bucket dripping a macabre, soapy mosaic into the blood pool. Two men were feet away, in heavy discussion with Jake Zobo. Billy joined their conversation.

"She wasn't watching where she was mopping. She slipped."

A manager interrupted in a lazy voice, "Were the safety cones near the perimeter of the boom lift?"

Billy's posture immediately became combative as Jake responded, "Em, em, she wasn't looking—"

The second manager asked, "What happened to your pump assembly assistant?" Jake ignored the question, still whining.

"I was working very hard when it happened," lamely crawled out of Jake, and Billy jumped in.

Were lock and tag-out keys not in place? If you had locked out the equipment, no one would have been able to operate the machine. You were trained to do that. Why didn't you lock it out?"

No response.

Billy lost it and got in Jake's face, shouting, "Where the fuck are the lock and key? Do you ever read goddamn company safety procedures?"

"I, I..." Jake stammered.

Billy's anger boiled over. "You lock the pumps out and attach the pump chain to the wall. Thus, the pump will not fall onto the floor if the boom lift fails. Yeah?"

"It was an acciden—"

"And if you'd tagged the pump, the poor woman would see the tag and not approach the area as they'd been trained. Asshole!" Billy admonished him relentlessly, the image of his dead janitorial mother not far from his mind.

"I wasn't thinking—" Jake began to say.

"Damn right, you weren't. So, the pump never locked & tagged out, the boom lift wasn't secured to the wall, your assistant was literally out to lunch, and you didn't cordon off the assembly area? It's manslaughter," Billy concluded in vehemence.

The two managers tried pulling Billy away from Jake.

Billy got back in Jake's face, trembling and on the verge of crying, and laid into him further.

"You're one useless piece of shit! Privileged motherfucker."

"But, but—"

"But, but what? Has your mother ever worked three jobs to provide for you? Course not. Your cock-sucking ass is here because it's your Pa's b-nez," Billy scolded.

The two managers grabbed Jake and walked the trembling adolescent off the factory floor. Billy chased after them.

After work, Billy was frazzled and went to a nearby park to de-stress.

As he sat down, he kept seeing the old janitor's body in the blood pool, imagining her to be his mother, Florence. She was also a janitor before the accident.

Billy briefly thought about calling Kyle and Sylvia, but cowardly out, convincing himself his isolation was for their benefit. It wasn't.

The following morning, the security guard stood outside the open door of Billy's office to watch him pack.

He pulled off wall plaques, selected files from drawers, scooped up desk mementos and Judy's portrait, dumped them all in a box, and closed the lid.

The security guard held the building's front entrance door open.

He walked through with the box after being fired.

He staggered into the apartment lounge with the box and halted in front of Judy, who was dressed on the sofa, seething.

Two suitcases were next to her.

She looked up at the wall clock: 2:20 a.m. She got in Billy's face, talking… "You're drunk and—"

"Hell to the fuck yes," Billy yelled back.

He dropped the box loudly beside the suitcases and walked towards the kitchen.

"Got fired today, and I'm pissed, angry, and—"

The front door slammed loudly and echoed through the apartment as he poured liquor. He spilled half of it and spun to see Judy and the suitcases gone.

"Bitch."

He staggered to the sofa, flopped, spilled more drinks, and passed out.

The cell phone ringing woke him up; he looked at the screen, and it was Kyle.

He ignored it, lay his head on the sofa, and soon began snoring.

***

Kyle had sequestered himself in Chinatown, Houston, in a hole-in-the-wall motel–House of Shih–hiding out for months since the robbery.

When Billy did not beep back, Kyle left him a couple of voicemails.

“Hey, bro, we all have this dark cloud of Jordan over our heads, but we’ve got to shake it. Don’t throw Sylvia and me away, Billy. We need you. I need you now. I’m in a jam.”

A week later, Kyle left another voicemail. “Please, help me, Billy.”

Billy never responded.

Kyle scoured newspapers daily and listened to the TV and the radio for news on the heist, but nothing showed. He began to gain confidence.

He walked to the front desk of the motel. “These headaches are killing me, Chan. You got any of those Chinese herbs for me?”

The desk clerk looked at Kyle’s right eye. “Go see the doctor, my friend. You got money?” Kyle walked away.

Chan called after him. “Wait, wait. Say I sent you.” The clerk gave Kyle a written note with a squiggle on it.

Kyle read the note. It was not in English. “What is this?”

The clerk pointed across the street to another motel.

"Funny," Kyle said as he walked out.

Kyle was surprised to walk into an ophthalmologist's office.

"I'm Doctor Ken Yamamoto."

"You're Japanese," Kyle accused him.

"Is that a crime?"

"I was… never mind." He gave him the note.

"That would be $300 upfront."

"You read Chinese too?"

"No. That was a Japanese note."

Kyle giggled, stood back, sized him up, and paid.

He then scanned the neat office, with its clean equipment, that belied the building's shabby exterior.

Doctor Ken invited him to sit. "Tell me how you got here."

Kyle explained the bump on his head, replacing the bullet with a bat.

"For a handsome man that should be in the movies with your looks, why would you let someone bat you in the face?"

Kyle laughed. "My facelift went wrong."

The doctor didn't find it funny. "How long ago?"

"Three months now," he lied.

"Why not go to the emergency or hos..."

"Really? $300?" Kyle fell into a foul mood.

"Okay, okay."

Kyle underwent a series of tests on the equipment for the next two hours. Then, the doctor returned.

"The good news is that you had a massive concussion. The bad news is I have to relieve the swelling, and it will leave a scar. Finally, you must wear a patch for three weeks to rest the eye or risk a longer-term bad prognosis."

"That it?"

"No. Fifteen hundred to do all that I explained, and prescription drugs for two months."

"Did that note the clerk wrote you pin me as a sucker?"

The doctor laughed. "No, he said to help you for free, that you're the only pale face that has never looked down on him since you came. It will not be free, but I will offer you a deep discount."

"You're shitting me?"

“No. You want the note back?”

“Yes.”

Kyle took the note. “When is the surgery?”

“Tomorrow morning. Be fasting.”

Kyle walked out.

***

In the southwest part of Houston, in Chinatown, Kyle Pearse, wearing an eye patch and carrying a bag, ducked into the Chang Pu laundromat's back-alley backdoor and went into the back room, where a fierce game of Pai Gow poker had been going on all evening.

It was midnight.

A lady vacated a seat for him at the four-man table.

A bored man in ramshackle attire approached Kyle and dumped a bag of chips at his feet. Kyle handed the man the bag he was carrying. The man peeked inside the bag to see small dollar bill bundles and walked away.

Kyle rearranged the chips to his liking. “Let’s skin this baby, guys,” he said.

They all looked up at him, wearing an eye patch.

“Even a one-eyed lion catches prey. A weak prey.” A player quipped.

“Put up or shut up, two eyes,” Kyle objected, throwing a handful of chips into the pot. A glass of neat liquor appeared in front of him.

He looked at the waitress in a tight cheongsam with double gun piping. Kyle whistled and threw her a chip, which she caught with a smile.

Four hours later, Kyle staggered out, losing the ten grand he had walked in with.

***

Eight months later, in Georgia, a gorgeous redhead, five foot ten, buxom, and pregnant, Sylvia Pearse sat smoking on the couch beside Alonzo in the backroom at Alladin.

The phone rang, and Alonzo picked it up.

“Hey,” Kyle said.

“That’s all you got, asshole?”

“Don’t be like that, Alonzo.”

“The only reason I didn’t come after you was because of your sister and...”

“I know. Can I explain?”

“Not to me, pal. Brass Nacchio wants you badly. You gotta come explain to him.”

“Am I safe?”

“No, but I’ll do all I can to keep you alive until your explanations.”

“When?”

“Asshole, like yesterday.” Alonzo hung up.

“Who was that?” Sylvia asked.

“No one. Pass me the smoke.”

She did and sat on his lap, with her pregnant belly, her back to him. She began to grind on him.

“I’m horny like crazy,” she said.

“Sure, you gonna have to start paying me for service…”

“Shut up and do me, gangster.”

***

Kyle’s drive back to Georgia was uneventful.

He contemplated turning back and disappearing as he drove through Louisiana, but he knew Sylvia would bear the brunt. He floored the gas pedal.

When he passed through Mississippi, he stopped at the last border gas station and had second thoughts again.

In Alabama, he practically talked to himself, arguing back and forth about the merits and demerits of his return. Sylvia won.

The subtle weather difference between Texas and Georgia was always amazing, but the climatic condition was the least concern on Kyle's mind as he drove across the state line.

"Louisiana, Mississippi, Alabama? Fuck me," he said as he parked after the long drive.

***

Blackie and Alonzo walked Kyle into Brass's lounge when he arrived in Atlanta.

Brass looked at Blackie, who turned to face Kyle. "I'm sorry, man!"

He punched Kyle with a hard left hook to the gut, followed by an uppercut to the jaw that sent Kyle reeling. His eye patch flew off, and he passed out.

He woke up in a chair.

"You put me in a bad business position, Kyle. But for Alonzo, you'd be dead. So, explain to me why keeping you alive benefits me."

Kyle began to explain the robbery, but Brass cut him off.

"It doesn't matter what transpired. Only two questions matter now."

Kyle rubbed his jaw and leaned forward.

Blackie, looking a tad remorseful, gave him a glass of liquor. Kyle downed it in a gulp and shivered.

"What?" Kyle asked.

"Will the bodies ever pop up?"

"No."

"And if it does pop up, I have your permission to turn you in," Brass said.

"No. I'll take my chances without you helping the Cops."

Brass laughed out loud and shook his head in amazement.

"You got guts, kid, but it's likely to kill you too."

"Thank you," Kyle said.

"Do you have my cut?" Brass asked.

"I have twenty grand."

Brass laughed, looking at Blackie and Alonzo, who joined in on the laughter.

"My cut was one hundred grand. What happened?" Kyle shrugged.

"So, why don't I kill you, take the twenty, and sell Sylvia to the Sheiks in Saudi Arabia?"

"Can I work it off?" Kyle suggested.

Brass flared up and paced. "Do I look like Walmart?"

"But killing me gains you nothing?" Kyle negotiated.

Brass returned to sit down. "You got some big brass on you..."

Brass laughed at his own name's jocular irony, which went over Alonzo and Blackie's heads. Kyle got it. He almost snickered but caught himself in time.

"What do you suggest, brainiac?" Brass glared at him.

"I know you deal Fentanyl and Coyote bodies," Kyle replied.

"What are you? DEA?" Brass laughed out loud and then said, "So?"

"I bring a load from Mexico to square me," Kyle suggested.

"And if you fail?" Kyle shrugged. Brass looked at Blackie again.

"Oh no, no, no... please, no more," Kyle begged. Brass waved Blackie off.

"Blackie will take you to my partner, Aguapa Mentaje, pronounced 'Men-Tah-Hay,' in Tijuana, whom he used to work for. I just did you a favor, telling you how to say his name. He's killed people for far less. Now, get the fuck out of my house."

Brass walked off the lounge as Kyle, Alonzo, and Blackie exited.

Chapter 4

Several aimless years went by for Billy. Now, he found himself on the main street in the Gaslamp quarter.

Mildly disheveled, he walked down the quarter into the bar and poured himself out hours later, a little shitfaced.

He crossed the main street and continued down the avenue, stopping ten yards past a building with a large blue sign.

He pondered and turned to re-read the building sign. He smiled in recognition—Father Joe's soup kitchen.

The next afternoon, he walked through Father Joe's soup kitchen. The front door opened into the dining area.

Father Joe was eating at the table with the others. He waved Billy to an empty spot at the table. "It's a blessed day, son," he said.

All faces at the table were deep into a healthy portion of food on Styrofoam plates.

Billy turned to face Father Joe. "You don't remember me, do you?"

"Do cows give milk?" the Father countered.

Father Fantone then pondered for seconds and pointed. "Sanatorium, Tent City."

A Styrofoam food plate appeared in front of Billy. Billy's smile was rueful at Father Joe.

Billy asked, "Cows?"

"Blessings nary stifles selfless giving. Benevolence is human," the Father said.

Billy looked up in confusion, "I have no idea what you said, but thank you," and quickly returned to the meal.

The Father announced, "You all can volunteer with us here. We want you to find it in your heart, but never out of guilt or pity."

Billy looked up again, locked eyes with Father Joe, and then looked away.

Father Joe frowned at the sudden recall of Billy's name.

"If you're not in a hurry. Billy, right?"

Billy was not smiling. "I'm not a cow."

Father Joe got serious. "We're all sheep in the eyes of the Lord. I want to catch up with you, Billy," the Father commanded. Billy shrugged.

The following afternoon, he was in Father Joe's office.

He sat across from him—Father Joe behind a modest desk in a cluttered room with files, papers, and posters.

“We opened here a year ago when the sanatorium shut down on the patient abuse class action suit. Did you hear about it?”

Billy frowned in ignorance. “Any money floating on the class action, Father?”

Father Joe tapped on his head. “Are you still having those nightmares?”

In surprise at his recall, Billy shook his head. “Why a soup kitchen?”

“Why not, son?”

Billy fidgeted. “I gotta go.”

Father Joe studied him. “I’d like to offer you a job here. Cooking position. Pay stipends!”

Billy frowned and snickered in surprise. “Do you plan on poisoning yourself along with your volunteers?”

“I have a great culinary coach. Think about it.”

They shook hands, and Billy walked out.

***

As the years rolled on, the siblings grew apart. Billy, specifically, remained in solitude.

On this nice summer evening, Billy went to the movies with a client he’d been working with on a commercial real estate project.

Billy stopped as they thronged from the San Diego Fashion Valley AMC theatre and looked back at the marquee. "Marvel's The Avengers premieres next week," he read aloud, smiled, and turned to Colt Brenton, his client.

"I'm coming to the premier next week. You're invited."

"I'd love to, Mister Pearse, but I'm flying my son to Catalina for the week."

"Good for you. I didn't know you flew."

"Since I was fifteen. I think better when I'm looking down from the sky."

"Like God?" Billy teased.

"Oh no, more like an eagle."

"I will call you with the numbers early tomorrow, Colt."

"Yes, sir, my brother has been on my case for that."

They arrived at the parking lot and parted ways.

Billy had been negotiating with another real estate company for weeks to secure a space for a restaurant that the Brenton brothers wanted.

Father Joe had insisted that Billy do something different besides volunteering and building his real estate business...

“Ever since you sold my mother’s property in Poughkeepsie, you haven’t slowed down a bit, have you, Billy?”

They were in the dining hall late in the evening when the soup hall had been cleared and swept, and dishes washed.

Billy sipped his tea. “I need to keep moving, like a shark, or I will sink.”

Father Joe, across the table, leaned back. Billy looked up and said, “Oh no. The talk, again.”

“Yes, Billy. You have to reach out to Kyle and Sylvia. Aren’t you curious how they’re doing?”

“I know exactly how and what those two idiots are doing.”

Father Joe perked up. “Oh?”

“Before Nana died… You remember Nana Bertha, right?”

“Yeah, yeah. I do,” the Father confirmed.

“She wrote me monthly on their progress, and I sent whatever I had to her, with strict instruction never to bring me up.”

“Why, Billy?”

“I was still lost and was rebuilding.”

"But things are looking up now. You have a successful real estate business with an office in a great part of San Diego, and you have me."

Billy reached for Father Joe's hand across the table and held it with both hands.

"Yes, I do have you, and I always worry about what would happen to me if something should happen to you," Billy confessed.

"There's only one way to solve that, Billy; forgive yourself and your siblings, and you'll have nothing to worry about."

Billy stood up, went to the cleric, kissed him on the head, and left.

"Call them, Billy, you'll feel better." Billy did not respond.

***

Kyle and Sylvia's lives in Georgia were emotionally fraught with constant nightmares when Billy first dropped them off.

Kyle initially coped by waking up early to mow the lawn, which had become hard brush rather than weeds. He soon got bored.

At night, his nightmares were the same with slight variations...

"Return the toy car, Jordan. I'm warning you."

Jordan ran past a sleeping Billy and his friend through the lounge onto the balcony.

As Kyle neared him, he jumped off the balcony, his face and hands waving at Kyle to rescue him.

Then, he face-planted onto the asphalt with blood splattering and limbs askew.

...Then Kyle jumped up from sleep in a cold sweat, heaving.

Months later, Kyle, walking in the nearby woods, carved a catapult and began killing tens of squirrels for no reason.

He woke up early, donned a jacket, and hunted for the sluggish vermin.

Meanwhile, Sylvia's nightmares comprised tens of dolls, similar to those belonging to Nana Bertha, but with Jordan's face suffocating her. She woke up in a cry when it first began.

But as the months progressed, she got control of the nightmares by waking up at their crescendo, skulking to the lounge, grabbing two or three dolls from Nana Bertha's stack, taking them to her room, and stabbing them to shreds.

Then, early in the mornings, she stuffed the shredded dolls deep below the garbage can before anyone woke up.

So, Kyle noticed Sylvia's early morning foray as he returned from his own squirrel-shooting one morning.

It then became routine for him to watch Sylvia dump the torn dolls. He retrieved and dumped them farther away from the ranch to avoid an accidental discovery by Nana Bertha, but he did not say a word to Sylvia.

It was early morning as Nana Bertha foot-pushed herself forward in her wheelchair towards the lounge door.

"Sylvia dear, are we ready to go?" "Yes, Nana. I'm putting on my face."

Nana snickered. "Where did your face go?"

"To my belly."

They both laughed as Sylvia pushed Nana out the door.

Sylvia now worked in a hair salon owned by Nana's long-time bingo friend. But the money Sylvia made only went so far, so she began hanging out with her salon coworkers who moonlighted at the local gentleman's club called Alladin.

At the doctor's office, Nana Bertha was warned again about eating sugar to curb her diabetes.

"Miss Bertha, if you don't reduce your sugar intake, your diabetes will affect your mobility further than it does now."

"You mean I'll be wheelchair-bound worse than I am now?" Nana jested.

Sylvia looked at the doctor expressionlessly, resting against the wall and filing her long, painted nails. The doctor challenged her.

"Young lady, you should cook healthy meals for your granny." Both Sylvia and Nana burst out laughing. Nana smiled at the Doctor.

"If I ate what that child cooks, I wouldn't need this damn wheelchair." Nana pointed to the heavens, confusing the Doctor.

"What?"

"I'll be dead," Nana confirmed.

The doctor wrote prescriptions as Sylvia gathered Nana Bertha's stuff to leave.

As they neared home, Nana Bertha asked, "The counselor visited me last evening while you were at work and said you haven't been to school in a week." Sylvia didn't answer.

"Is that true, child?"

"I'm not learning anything; I need to make money."

Nana forcefully halted her movement by putting her foot down. "What do you need the money for?"

Sylvia stepped in front of her, akimbo, although respectfully. "Kyle and I will not live with you forever. We must save if we have to get a place."

"You're only sixteen. How long have you had this thought in your head, Sylvia?

"Always, Nana. Kyle is twenty-one. I always worry about what Kyle and I will do when we no longer live here." "You mean when I'm dead?" Nana asked.

Sylvia kneeled, hugged, and kissed Nana on the cheek. "You're too mean to die, Nana Bertha."

They both laughed and wheeled on.

Three years later, Nana Bertha died from chronic diabetes two months after both her legs were amputated above the knees.

By then, Kyle had dropped out of school, joined a gang, and worked in a garage. Kyle was twenty-four, and Sylvia was nineteen.

Kyle and Sylvia rented a one-bedroom apartment after the bank threw them out, as Nana Bertha's home was mortgaged to the hilt. Nana had been living off the shady reverse mortgage equity withdrawals and gradually losing her ownership.

Kyle slept in the lounge pull-down bed while Sylvia had the room. They battled daily over how long Kyle would keep the lounge decent for their friends to visit.

Sylvia won all the fights. Soon, Kyle began sleeping at home less and less.

At the garage, Kyle met Alonzo Gaza, who brought a Camaro to be souped up. After Kyle finished the upgrade, Alonzo invited him to an illegal street race where they did wheelies before the event.

Alonzo welcomed the handsome Kyle Pearse with a cleft chin to an abandoned farm with tarred roads. "Hey. You made it."

Cars of various designs revved and played, generating white smoke everywhere. Alonzo threw the Camaro keys at Kyle. "Well, grease monkey?"

Kyle jumped into the car without hesitation and pulled off ten consecutive wheelies with all of Alonzo's posse clapping.

"You're pretty goddamn good, boy?" Alonzo commended.

"If it's got wheels..." Kyle trailed off.

Alonzo asked, "You wanna try your hand at a race later?"

"Too rich for my blood." Kyle hesitated.

"Five bills too rich for you?" Alonzo asked in surprise.

"I got responsibilities, man."

Alonzo shot him a look. "You got kids or something?"

"No. I got a sister I gotta take care of."

"Oh?" Alonzo asked.

"She works at a salon," Kyle said, as if that justified anything.

Alonzo smiled. "Is she choosy about what she does?"

"What do you mean?"

Alonzo smiled.

"I run the only decent club in this hole of a walled town."

"Alladin?" Kyle asked.

Alonzo giggled. "Are you a customer?"

"I dabble," Kyle confirmed.

Then, the race lined up, and Alonzo threw the Camaro keys at Kyle. "You win; you keep the money."

"And if I lose?" Kyle asked.

"Introduce me to your sister, and we're squared."

Kyle won the race.

A month later, Kyle introduced Sylvia to Alonzo anyway.

Alonzo, in turn, hinted at a getaway drive job to Kyle…

Chapter 5

A black car idled behind a Texas Houston bank building in the late afternoon.

Skinny Kyle Pearse, twenty-four, was restless at the wheel.

"C'mon, c'mon," he mouthed. The door behind the bank burst open.

Two men, one in a face mask and one without, rushed out, each lugging a heavy black bag and wielding guns.

Kyle revved and pulled a fast U-turn, tires smoking. He lined up with the bank's back door. All three bank robbers scrambled into the car.

Tall and angular, Trevor Russo, without a face mask, yelled, "Let's get the hell out of here." Kyle took off.

A uniformed security guard bursts out of the bank door, firing at the getaway car, rapidly gunning down the alley.

At the main road, away from being shot, Les Smith, with a mean scar across his right cheek, mouthed off, "You motherfucking bastards just sent me back to the joint!"

Fat Dave Pelt, beside him in the back seat, yelled at Trevor. "Fucking amateur. Why in the hell would you take off your mask, Trevor? I warned you about candid cameras."

Les Smith also yelled at Trevor, "I should have listened to your Pa, Trevor. You ain't ready for this shit."

Kyle, speeding over 100 miles per hour, floored the pedal even further, zigzagging around cars as he headed for the outskirts of town. "Y'all shut the fuck up before I drive your ass into a goddamn ditch."

"Shut up and drive, asshole. You ain't paid to—" Trevor began to say. Kyle screeched to a slow, then a crawl, and was about to stop. "You wanna repeat that motherfucker?"

Les Smith calmed Kyle down. "Come on, Kyle. Trevor is nothing but a dick nozzle." "I better not hear any pee come out that nozzle, boy." Kyle threatened.

"Motherfucking drive already," Les encouraged.

"We cool?" Kyle asked Trevor. "We're cool. Now hitch this wagon on fast," Trevor responded. Kyle floored it.

He sharply turned off the main road, heads banging against car panels. He looked in the rearview mirror. No one chasing slowed down to a normal pace.

"Took the mask off 'cause I couldn't see," Trevor confessed. "That tends to happen when you wear it backward, dumbass," Les admonished. "You shut the fuck up. I'm warning you!" Trevor boomed.

A desolate industrial property appeared ahead. Kyle headed for it.

Kyle drove behind an abandoned warehouse in the late afternoon. He pulled up just short of a collection of rusty drums next to a grimy pond lit by street lights from the other side of the lake.

Face masks now off, the bank robbers yelled at each other continuously inside the car. All three jumped out.

Trevor walked away from the other two, waving a gun haphazardly and mumbling, “Motherfucker. Motherfucker.”

Trevor turned around and charged Les and Dave. When they saw him coming, they ran away toward the parked car.

“I’ll kill you. I’ll kill you!” Trevor yelled, firing at them. Dave and Les scrambled to hide around the car.

All three were now running, ducking, weaving, and firing at each other in a full gunfight around the car.

Kyle’s head was down on the driver's side seat as bullets flew around the vehicle. He raised his head cautiously to sneak a peek.

A stray bullet grazed his temple. Now bleeding, he flattened further onto the passenger seat, blood seeping into his eyes as he passed out.

The gunfight slowed down with moans and groans until everything went eerily quiet.

It was dark when Kyle regained consciousness, holding his head. His hand came off bloody as he sat up with blurry vision in both eyes, but the right eye was almost shut. He looked out of the shattered window when his vision cleared up.

He slowly exited the car and walked around to see Dave, Les, and Trevor lying dead. He kicked them to be sure.

He searched for a place to stash or bury the bodies but settled on six rusty drums on a pallet.

He rolled over three drums and found a sharp iron rod to punch holes in the sides of all three.

He stuffed Dave, Les, and Trevor into each drum, then covered them with lever lock ring lids.

Now sweating profusely, he rolled the drums into the lake, watched them float for a while, and then gradually sank as air bubbles escaped from the drum side holes.

He collected all the guns, opened the car boot, and replaced the spare tire with them.

He pulled money bags from the car and opened them, revealing plenty of small-dollar bills. Exhausted, he placed the bags on top of the guns in the trunk.

Drenched with sweat, he took off minutes later.

As he drove, his vision alternated between blurry and clear. He stopped at a gas station to make a call.

“Hi, Billy, it’s me, Kyle. I need your help, not for money, but to lay low for a while. Please, beep me at this number…” Billy never called Kyle back.

Billy, soaked, was walking home from a bar when Kyle’s call came.

Once the voicemail was completed, he listened and burst out in self-deprecating laughter, smelling his breath for the heavy alcohol smell.

“I can hardly help myself, kid. I can only bring you more grief, Kyle. I’m sorry,” he said as he drunk-staggered on the empty road at 1 am.

***

Alonzo asked Sylvia what she wanted to do as they had a meal at a dive in Georgia. “You ever pole-danced?”

“You mean like a hooker?” she asked.

“Dancers dance and hookers hook.”

“I ain’t either of those things.”

“So, what are you?”

“I work in a salon and wanna be a nurse.”

“Don’t you have to go to school for that?”

"Yeah, I plan to." She hesitated and added, "Once I put the money together."

"How can I help?" Alonzo asked.

She smiled. "Kyle said to be careful of you."

Alonzo pointed at his heart. "I'm offended. I thought we were friends."

Sylvia smiled. "How much do dancers make?"

Alonzo said with a faraway look, "Depends on what you're willing to do."

"Like what?"

"Why don't you come and see for yourself tonight? I'll pick you up."

After a moment, Sylvia decided, "Okay."

Chapter 6

Sylvia watched the dancers in skimpy outfits suggestively gyrate on the poles with dollar bills stuck into their dental floss panties.

Alonzo, circulating as the host, discreetly watched her reactions. He sidled over to her.

"They're very brave," she charged.

"Why?"

"Wearing next to nothing and having money shoved up your ass."

"Making two bills a night ain't bad."

"Two hundred dollars a night? It takes me a week to clear 200 with OT." Alonzo shrugged and walked away.

A month later, Sylvia was gyrating on the pole nightly while working her day job at the salon.

Two months after she began dancing at the Aladdin, Sylvia moved in with Alonzo.

She was in his apartment lounge, shooting up. "Hey, babe, don't burn it all up; leave me some," he called from the bedroom.

She lay back on the couch, and her eyes glazed over as the injected heroin took effect.

Alonzo walked in, pecked her forehead, sat beside her, and began cooking the stuff on a silver spoon.

Six months after living together, Alonzo suggested a scheme to make enormous amounts of money to fund her nursing ambitions.

In one of their sober moments, he asked, “You ever wanna have children?” “Never,” was the immediate, unflinching answer she gave.

“Wow. You sound mad.” He said.

“Tell me one good thing about having a child.”

“You’re kidding, right?” he asked.

She faced him squarely. “No. Plead your case.”

“They love you, make life worth living, take care of you in your old age, they…”

She put up her hand for him to stop. “Tell me one thing,” she asked honestly.

“Yeah?” He leaned in closer to her.

“Can anyone guarantee those things will happen?”

He reared back. “No.”

“So?” she questioned and lit a joint. “My brother Jordan died, splat on a fucking asphalt after five years of my mother investing in him for all those promises you said. I ain’t ever having kids.”

Alonzo moved tightly next to her. “What if you get paid doing it and don’t even have to care for the child one day?”

“That’s crazy talk,” she said, pulling hard on the weed.

“No. I got a connection. Ten grand for a nine-month work and no babies to fuck with afterward.”

“I’m tired, Alonzo. Come with me to the bedroom. We're gonna play mommy and daddy.” She walked off, and he ran after her.

“You don’t have to ask me twice,” he said.

***

Brass Nacchio, who looked like a school principal and was in his fifties, had his hands in everything around Georgia.

He’d risen in the underground Fentanyl business in Atlanta over the years. His ties to the Mexican Cartel were well documented. He had juice within the local law enforcement agencies.

Recently, he dived into human trafficking of the worst kind, selling newborn babies cultivated with willing pregnancy mules.

Alonzo walked into Brass's back room in the affluent Druid Hills neighborhood of Atlanta, into a room behind the kitchen where four people were gambling on a green velvet poker table.

"Sit down, Alonzo, and stop hovering over my head."

Alonzo pulled up a chair and sat feet behind Brass.

"No need to introduce everyone, right, Alonzo?"

"Nah."

Blackie, a blonde guy, nodded at Alonzo, who nodded back. It was unclear why a blonde, blue-eyed dude would be named Blackie.

Fat Wendell Allshot, Brass's accountant, grunted when Alonzo looked at him. He went back to repeatedly swapping the card positions in his hand.

As they played, Brass asked. "Is that the carrier outside?"

"Yeah."

"And she knows the deal?"

"I've been grooming her for a year."

"That's not what I asked, compadre."

"Yes, she knows the deal," Alonzo confirmed.

Brass stopped playing, stood up, and faced the other players."

"Deal me out on the next hand."

He pulled Alonzo up and led him outside the kitchen into the lounge. Sylvia hears them coming and hides until they enter a room.

"Alonzo, women are very strange animals. They're not like men. So, when I asked, did she know her baby would be taken the minute she had him? You'd better be sure."

"I'm sure, boss."

"So, how long is left in the oven?"

"A couple of months."

They both went back to the poker game room. Sylvia avoided them again.

When the coast was clear, she entered a secluded corner of the lounge. At the cove, an old, short, golden scimitar in its sheath lay on the desk near a black-and-white picture frame.

She picked up the picture for a closer look. Brass Nacchio, Blackie, and Wendell Allshot in front of a golf clubhouse, with names penciled under each image.

She heard a door opening and hurried back into the lounge. She bumped into Alonzo.

“What did I tell you about wandering around?”

She laughed sheepishly and followed him out of the lounge.

Alonzo drove off Nacchio’s compound.

Sylvia rolled down the window on the Highway and dropped the short scimitar.

“What’d I tell you about the fucking window?”

“I’m pregnant, you know?”

He flashed a look that conveyed, “So what?” He smiled instead.

Five months in, her pregnancy not yet showing, Alonzo smiled at Sylvia Pearse as she pranced on stage atop unbelievably high heels, then ground on the center shiny dance pole. Men waved dollar bills to edge her on.

***

Alonzo sensed eyes on him. He turned around and looked in Blackie’s direction. Blackie glided away smoothly, deeper into the club.

Blackie tapped on an older black stripper’s shoulder, walking by with a drinks tray. “Lap dance?” “Fuck off,” she said.

Blackie moved on and walked past a patron in the corner seat. A topless, skimpy girl was butt-grinding on the patron. The patron stuffed dollar bills into her panties.

On stage, Sylvia finished her dance, moved to the edge of the stage, and stooped low for the men to stuff dollar bills into her low, pink V-cut panties.

Alonzo walked over and, with great care, guided Sylvia off stage.

"I'm hot, baby," she said.

Both walked off towards the club's backroom. Sylvia is in front.

"I know you're hot," Alonzo smiled.

"No, no, no. Not that. I mean, I'm burning up." She complained.

"Come on then."

Alonzo unlocked the backroom door.

Sweatily clammy, Sylvia collapsed on the sofa next to her small purse.

Alonzo lit a joint on another sofa across the center table from Sylvia.

She sat up and urged him to pass the joint over. He looked at her belly and hesitated briefly. Sylvia looked where he was looking. "You, my Mama?" She challenged. He passed the joint over to her.

She grabbed her purse with the joint in her mouth, fished inside the purse, and placed a small mirror on the center table.

She spread white powder lines from a vial onto the mirror, inhaled two lines loudly, and rubbed her pregnant belly.

Alonzo inhaled the remaining two lines, wiped the mirror with a finger, dabbed his gum with the index finger, got up, sat beside Sylvia, and held her hand.

Both rested their heads on the sofa blissfully.

Chapter 7

Three and a half months later, in the lounge of their apartment, burst-at-any-minute pregnant Sylvia Pearse was sluggish as she snorted cocaine from a mirror on the center table.

"I wish this bitch would get out of me," She lamented.

Alonzo, her boyfriend, looked up, toked on a fat joint, and watched with disgust at the powder dust around Sylvia's nostrils as her head slowly slumped back on the sofa's backrest.

He crushed the joint in the ashtray, bent over the mirror, snorted lines, and came back up for air.

"Ain't you too... to still be doing that shit?" he asked.

Sylvia's head snapped up with venom. "Back the fuck off, asshole."

Alonzo Mea Culpa shrugged. "I'm just saying."

She screamed and waddled upright from the sofa as amniotic fluid dribbled down between her legs.

He fell off the sofa in disbelief, seeing her peeing herself, and then realized it wasn't pee.

"Motherfucker." He cursed as he rushed to the kitchen wall phone, dialed 911, and ran out of the lounge.

In the bedroom, he haphazardly hid drugs, guns, and heaps of dollar bills on the bedside table, then heard her scream-yell again. “Get the fuck back here!”

Back in the lounge, he leaned her carefully against the wall as the siren noise got louder.

He pried her hands off him to clean cocaine powder off the table and to dump the ashtray formerly filled with weed stubs.

He sprayed the room with a rose-scented canister and returned to care for her.

They both started to whoosh-breathe, in and out in unison, awaiting the ambulance.

Sylvia lost the baby.

Three months later, after the loss of her pregnancy, Sylvia had cleaned up nicely and sat beside Alonzo at the adoption agency.

Red-eyed, she and her boyfriend leaned across the desk toward the adoption agent.

Sylvia addressed the female agent. “We feel so blessed and can’t wait to—” The agent raised a hand and spoke gently. “I know how eager we all are, but—”

The door opened, and a male agent joined the meeting.

“I’m here to remind you and reinforce elements of your counseling sessions and to reconfirm your resolve remained strong as the process neared conclusion.”

Sylvia smiled sadly. “Yes, our resolve is crystal clear. I’m neither impulsive nor substituting for my lost pregnancy. Alonzo and I are motivated to nurture, love, and prepare a better combined human version of ourselves for society.”

Alonzo added, “It’s not lost on us that we must manage expectations and be wary of potential strains on our relationships. But we are ready.” He held Sylvia’s hand tightly.

Both agents nodded in agreement.

The female agent said, “Now we get to the most critical aspects of your presence today.” She looked at the male agent.

“We have a six-month-old boy from a deceased single mother, lost to cancer, without any other relatives. The boy is healthy and vibrant.”

Sylvia started crying. “I, I, I—” Alonzo reached for her hand. “It’s okay, baby.”

The agent continued, “The judge must now analyze your circumstances and decide upon your qualifications. Are you old enough? Are you financially secure enough to provide lifetime support?

“Do you both possess the staying power to prepare a child’s growth that enables him to navigate severe physiological, neurological, and behavioral challenges thrown at him? These are what's at stake."

Sylvia's dry face showed a firm resolve. "We know that, immediately, the child will fuss and fret as he suffers and experiences changes when we hold him close, and we plan to be there every day, every hour as necessary. We're ready, as our psychological profile assessments indicated."

Alonzo confirmed, "We're ready."

The female agent breathed a loud sigh of relief. "Now then, all that's left is for the judge to decide, but before then, we need to hear from your eldest brother as a guarantor."

Sylvia's demeanor shifted, which she hid instantly. "Why wouldn't my other sibling, Kyle, guarantee us?"

Both agents looked at each other, and the male agent spoke, "He has a record." Sylvia sat up straighter.

"Okay, we'll call Billy." She then leaned in. "Can we see the baby?"

"I'm afraid you'll have to wait until the judge approves all your legal orders."

Sylvia and Alonzo held hands, looked into each other's eyes, and nodded. They turned to the agents. "We're ready."

“Hi, Billy. I’ve never asked you for anything over the years, but now I need you. I’m going through an adoption process. Please stand as my guarantor. Please tell me you accept. Thank you.” Billy never called back.

She dialed Kyle’s number and then hung up before it went through.

Predictably, the adoption fell through.

Billy, on the phone, worked behind his second-floor office desk in a thin slice of heaven. He can see the Pacific Beach Ocean from his Pacific Beach Real Estate office window.

He talks and stares at wall portraits—real-estate commendation plaques alongside a framed picture of himself with Father Joe Fantone.

“I promise I won’t be late. Yes. 5:00 p.m. tonight, but I gotta stop downtown for a couple of hours first.”

He listened and then continued, “No. I have to be downtown first. I promise I’ll be on time. La Jolla, right? Gotta go.”

He dropped the call, checked items off a large wall calendar, adjusted his tie, grabbed his jacket from a coat hanger, and left the office with a smile and a briefcase.

It was a bright sunny afternoon when Billy, in a suit, walked into Father Joe's soup kitchen.

He entered the kitchen and saw eighteen-year-old Garcia Lopez stirring a large pot on the stove.

He asked the kid. "Are you on schedule for the onslaught coming tonight?"

"Yes and no, Yo."

Billy stared hard at the young man. "Don't call me Yo." The kid giggled endearingly.

Billy peeled off his jacket, loosened his tie, rolled his sleeves, and retrieved the chopping board near the sink. He then opened the refrigerator for vegetables, washed his hands, and began chopping.

Garcia smiled at him. "I'm sorry I Yo'd you, jefe! It won't happen again." Billy chuckled. "Knucklehead." His cell phone rang.

He wiped off his hands and pulled out the phone. It was Kyle, his brother. He ignored it.

Two hours later, now dark outside, his jacket back on, he walked out the front door and listened to cellphone messages; as he walked, Kyle's message was first.

"At some point, you'll have to let us in, Billy. I know you want to; otherwise, you'd have changed your number all these years, but you didn't. What will it take, Bro? Call your sister Sylvia. She's not doing so great with her boyfriend!"

Billy's head drooped in sadness as he trudged down the avenue.

At the La Jolla Village Square Mall, he opened the door into a large commercial shopfront, and a vast, empty floor space greeted him.

Slim and agile Colt Brenton, thirty-three, rushed over and pumped his hand enthusiastically.

"Man, I was on pins and needles."

Billy was equally enthusiastic and man-hugged Colt.

Stocky Hayden Brenton, two years older than his brother Colt, walked over with a smile, hands spread wide to illustrate the vastness of space. "Heyyy... we did it."

Billy walked over to the table in the middle of the space, to a champagne bottle in an ice bucket next to three flutes.

He popped the cork and filled the flutes with massive gas bubbles overflowing.

The Brenton brothers joined him, picked up drinks, and raised glasses in a toast. "To the Maori Brenton brothers."

"To Billy Pearse, the best commercial real estate agent in San Diego."

"From your mouth to god's ears, partner."

Glasses clinked, and Hayden downed a single flute.

Colt contemplated aloud, "So, what happens now?

Billy laughed and drank. "Nothing, man. Build your opus. Your masterpiece is what's next."

Colt locked eyes with Hayden and paused. "All right then. Haka-Liki, here we come."

Colt Brenton piloted a Cessna 172 over Canyons & Gorges in Southern California.

The upbeat Salsa tune "Betece " by Amadou Balake energized Hudson Brenton on the passenger side as he rocked to the music.

Speaking into a microphone attached to his headphones, he pointed down. "Look, Dad."

Colt Brenton nodded as horses in corrals frolicked in farms and villages.

The aerial view shifted to showcase lakes and the beachfront. It sets San Diego apart from other cities.

Colt got serious over the microphone. "Hudson, I'm glad you came with me to Catalina. I've missed this."

"Yeah, Dad. I wish Uncle Hayden had come with us. He would..."

Colt interrupted in anger... "This has nothing to do with Hayden. It's a father and son thing!"

Hudson brooded and turned off the music. "I wish you and Uncle Hayden would settle this thing, whatever it is, between you."

"He's my brother, but cannot steal my son from under my nose."

Hudson became angry. "Let's go home, Dad. I'm not a trinket, you know?"

Colt did not back down. "You're my trinket, pal!"

Already on the descent, the small aircraft sighted the San Diego International Airport on the horizon.

***

In Atlanta, Georgia, Kyle was on his way to Tijuana, Mexico, to pay off his debt to Brass Nacchio.

He was in a car with Brass's henchman, Blackie, a five-foot-nine stocky hombre with a penchant for black cowboy boots.

Kyle looked at his feet. "How can you drive with that thing?"

"Just stick your foot out, Einstein."

And that kicked off what would become a memorable journey.

Blackie, at the wheel of the Classic Cutlass Supreme, merged into traffic heading to Tijuana.

"No hard feelings about the..." He touched his jaw and quickly looked at Kyle as he drove.

Kyle also rubbed his jaw. "You didn't have to hit so hard."

"That wasn't hard, trust me." "Bullshit," Kyle said.

"Have you ever been in a cage fight?" "Were you?" Kyle asked. "That's where Brass recruited me."

"So, I should fucking thank you for not breaking my jaw?"

"You're welcome."

"Asshole." Kyle cursed.

In Shreveport, Louisiana, Blackie pulled into a gas station at the border town.

"You wanna drive?"

"Nah, just wanna sleep and heal my whole body you pummeled," Kyle whined.

"Are you ever gonna let go of that?" "No. Not until payback."

Blackie laughed. "The day you beat me up is the day I have a sex change."

Kyle snapped him a look as Blackie exited the car. Kyle yelled after him. "Fine by me, buttercups."

Blackie gave him the finger as he walked into the food mart.

Kyle was now driving.

"Why would anyone call a white guy like you Blackie?"

Blackie turned to sneer at him. "You jealous?"

"No. Curious."

"It was dramatic." Blackie shut down the curiosity, but Kyle wouldn't let it go.

"I've never known you not to wanna blow your own horn."

Blackie, chewing on beef jerky, put both feet on the dashboard.

"You haven't known me that long."

"Long enough," Kyle said, rubbing his jaw.

Minutes elapsed, and Kyle went back to the Blackie question.

"So, what's the story??

Blackie blew his top and grabbed the steering wheel as Kyle was cruising at 100 miles per hour.

The car swerved and went off-road. The saving grace was that they were in the middle of nowhere, and the next cars were slower behind them.

Kyle struggled to control the car, and they ended up in a ditch.

The car stalled, and they were both now bleeding in the mouth, having banged their faces onto the dashboard, and sat quietly.

Blackie thrust the piece of beef jerky in his hand at Kyle. “You want a bite?”

Kyle exited the car to check the tires. It was stuck in a muddy gap. He returned to Blackie’s window.

“You're gonna have to push while I stir.”

Ten minutes later, they were back on the road, and Kyle was still driving.

“You wanna tell me what all that back there was about?”

“What?”

“Driving us into the ditch, asshole?”

“You wouldn’t let go, that’s what!”

“You’re crazy,” Kyle retorted.

"I wouldn't use that term again if I were you," Blackie cautioned.

They drove quietly to Fort Worth, Dallas.

"I'm tired," Kyle complained.

Chapter 8

Blackie, now driving, popped a soda can and offered it to Kyle, who looked at him suspiciously.

"Is that your apology? You should concentrate on driving."

"Yes, I apologize, but don't be bugging me anymore, okay?" Kyle took the peace offering.

"Just drive, Blackie, and no more shit."

Blackie laughed out loud and slapped the dashboard.

"That's what I'm talking about," he said as he dangerously overtook a truck that blasted its horn at them. It was midnight.

By the time they got to the border town in Tucson, Arizona, Blackie pulled into a secluded gas station at noon.

"I'll be right back." He walked off before Kyle could tell him to turn the engine off.

"What an asshole," Kyle muttered as he exited the car himself, the engine still running.

He walked behind the food mart to stretch his legs.

He then looked left and right, saw no one, and began to pee on the wall.

When done, he strolled towards the car, whistling at his mischief.

The food mart door busted open as Kyle neared the passenger side door. Blackie yelled, running.

"Drive, drive..."

Kyle instinctively went to the driver's side and got in as shots rang out from the now-opened food mart door at Blackie, who was ducking and weaving.

Kyle gunned the engine, pulled a donut to position the passenger door at Blackie while shielding him from the flying bullets.

Blackie jumped in through the open window as Kyle took off, Blackie's legs dangling outside the window.

Kyle hit the Highway, brushed a car lightly, straightened up, and gassed it.

Blackie, now fully in the car, was roaring, adrenaline-fueled laughter. "Holy shit, I almost got my ass shot off."

He looked at Kyle. "Man, I'm glad I didn't hit you too hard back in Atlanta."

Now out of danger, Kyle slowed down and switched to the right lane. "You wanna tell me what all that back there was about?"

Blackie took out a bunch of crumpled dollar bills and tossed them all over a furious Kyle. “I robbed the till, but there wasn’t much in there.”

Kyle was in utter confusion. “Did you need the money?”

Blackie shot him a glance as if he were stupid. “No. It was for fun.”

Kyle could only shake his head as they saw the sign for Mexicali. “You’re crazy.”

Blackie turned serious, his neck stiff as he spoke. “I told you not to call me that.”

“You almost got us killed.”

“So? You never know when death is going to come, so never pussy out.”

“You gone Zen?”

“Pull over,” Blackie commanded. Kyle kept driving.

“I ain’t gonna ask you again.”

Kyle crash-parked on a graveled patch and slammed the brakes. “What the fuck, man?” Kyle asked in anger.

Blackie turned to Kyle and undid the top button of his shirt, revealing a pendant that read “Blackie.”

Kyle, in confusion, gave him a questioning look.

"I had this big black Labrador back in Kansas. When I was two, my parents' ranch burned down with them in it. My dog, Blackie, was burning, but he pulled me outside to safety and went back inside. He died. In his honor, I officially changed my name to Blackie. I've never told that story to anyone before. Now drive." Kyle was stunned.

They arrived at Aguapa Mentaje's home two hours later.

***

Valle de las Palmas – Tijuana, México

Seventy-year-old Aguapa Mentaje remained as sharp as ever, having parlayed his fifty-year streetwise chicanery and brutal treatment of his competition into the second-largest Fentanyl supplier in Mexico.

His jet-black hair contrasted with his white mustache, making him look like a Mariachi. The persona had lulled many a foe to their demise.

Blackie led Kyle into the palatial homestead in the sprawling hacienda at the top of a hill in Valle de Las Palmas, surrounded by nothing. The next home was miles away.

Several large structures dotted the hacienda.

Aguapa, with a wide smile, welcomed Blackie. "¿Cómo está, mi amigo?"

"Bien, jefe, ¿y tú?" Blackie responded, hugging the older man.

Aguapa walked away without a look at Kyle.

The older man switched to perfect English. "How long are you staying?"

"Depends on you, boss."

Aguapa led them to an airy dining room with strong Spanish décor. The table was laden with delights, and they both sat.

Kyle also went to sit; Aguapa shot him a nasty look. Kyle retreated and stood in a corner, away from them.

"¿Por qué no se lo damos de comer a los perros ahora y reducimos nuestras pérdidas?" Aguapa suggested.

Kyle's eyes darted around, oblivious to what was just said.

"I think he can prove useful. He has heart." Blackie thumped his heart.

"He's too good-looking. I don't trust straight, good-looking men in my house," Aguapa concluded.

Valencia Mentaje, Aguapa's only child, a beautiful, tall, delicate woman, walked up and sat beside her father.

She ate a piece of meat that Aguapa was about to put in his mouth. She turned to face Blackie. "Hola, hombre blanco. ¿Cómo estás?"

“De nada, mi querida,” Blackie responded.

“Your Spanish sucked less, Blackie, Bienvenido,” Valencia commended.

“Gracias, Valencia,” Blackie responded.

Valencia looked at Kyle hanging about. “¿Quién es ese hombre guapo?”

Aguapa lost his shit and got up. Valencia rubbed his arm. He sobered instantly and sat.

Kyle patted his fingernails with his head down, oblivious to the goings-on.

Valencia waved him over. He didn’t see her gesture.

“Hey,” she called. Kyle looked up and hesitated until Aguapa nodded.

Kyle took a seat as far away from Aguapa as possible. He didn’t touch a thing as they all ate.

“Don’t you eat?” Valencia asked.

Kyle began to shovel down anything his hands landed on; Valencia laughed at his voraciousness.

“Hambre hombre.” She laughed at her joke.

“That’s going to be your name now. HH,” she said, laughing.

“What?”

Kyle looked up from stuffing his face, only to see all three looking at him like a caveman.

"I was hungry, man!" Kyle's first words since he entered the hacienda.

"Es un animales," Aguapa observed.

Everyone laughed except Kyle, who looked around, asking, "What? What'd he say?"

Martinez, Aguapa's Chemist and foreman, managed the Fentanyl factory in blue dungarees and a white T-shirt.

He walked through the concealed steel door inside a large warehouse beside a small cottage on Aguapa's Valle de Las Palmas hacienda, Tijuana.

Martinez lived at the cottage with his father and sister. They moved there from Van Nuys, California, six years earlier.

He scanned the compounding and packaging activities on the manufacturing floor and saw four Albino dwarfs at work.

He recruited the quadruplet Albinos from a circus that had come to a nearby village a year earlier. They were from Alaska, and all wore Peruvian Alpaca caps with tassels on either end.

Martinez made each Albino wear a different-colored hat to aid identification.

He talked to Short Albino1, wearing a red cap and a white lab coat, climbing a steel ladder attached to a 60-liter compounding vessel on wheels.

"Do you know how they catch monkeys in Brazil?" Martinez yodeled to the Albino.

Short Albino1, now on the vessel platform, clicked the lights button to see a thick, blue, viscous mixture inside the vessel and flipped the mixer switch on the vessel panel.

"That's what I'm talking about," he said as he climbed down, only to see Martinez walking towards him. They lock eyes. Martinez made hand signals to indicate, "I'm watching you."

Yards away, minutes later, Martinez rested his back against the wall, facing the steel door entrance, and observed Short Albino2, in a blue cap, operating a rotary tablet press.

Short Albino2 looked up and watched Martinez inspect blue tablets from the presser. "Hey, Martinez, do you know how they catch mon—"

"Shut the hell up," Martinez snapped and walked towards the conveyor, packing operations against the steel door's right wall.

A female Short Albino3 in a pink cap saw him and smiled eagerly. He hurried up towards her. "We gon party later?" He asked.

Short Albino3 smiled, showing two missing upper front gum teeth, as she applied tape to close corrugated boxes coming down the conveyor belt. "Por supuesto, jefe."

A Short Albino4 in a black cap was loading boxes onto pallets at the end of the conveyor belt when he stopped to look at them talking.

Packages backed up on the conveyor belt began to fall off noisily. Martinez turned to look and stormed towards the box pile-up.

"Pendejo estupido."

Short Albino4 crouched on the floor, picking up blue tablets that spilled everywhere.

Aguapa, Martinez's boss, followed by Blackie and Kyle, walked up to Martinez, who was about to hit Short Albino4.

Aguapa loudly yelled out, "¿ Qué paso, Martinez?"

Martinez's hand froze up mid-air. He turned to the voice and reluctantly walked towards Aguapa, who glared menacingly.

"Amable, por favor." The boss admonished.

Three hours later, outside, a truck pulled up in front of the cottage to the side of the manufacturing Fentanyl building.

The truck driver's hand rested on the horn button, blasting away. The thick-necked bodyguard beside him was expressionless.

Fully dressed, Martinez lay on the bed after a brief siesta, cringing as the loud horn blast permeated the air.

"Puta."

Still in the truck, hands now off the horn button, the driver yelled loudly at a toothless older man on the porch rocking chair, liquor in hand.

"How's it hanging, old-gringo."

"Like a church bell, drug dealer," the old man replied, not missing a beat. The driver giggled boisterously.

"I'm the driver to all the Pharmacists in the pueblo. I am a willing, ready, and able old man."

The older man gave him the finger. "You can kiss my Avocado, dickhead."

The driver smiled as he drove towards the shed behind the cottage.

Martinez rolled off the bed, put on hi-top sneakers, slid a small knife into the right shoe, and walked out and saw Kyle walking towards him.

"Hola," he said. "Hello," Kyle replied.

The driver walked towards Short Albino1 in the Meth lab at the left room corner, dumping a liquid drum into a compounding vessel. He turned to talk to the bodyguard. He was not there.

"Hey, Hey. What the hell?"

As soon as they entered the lab, the bodyguard spun, looked, and froze as if something was amiss. He walked back towards the driver, his face shocked.

"What in the hell is going on here?"

The driver was confused by the bodyguard's tone.

"You high or something?"

The bodyguard pointed as he looked in the room. "They're all short, Albinos."

The driver deflated with disappointment. "Your point?"

The bodyguard shuddered. "It's just weird."

The driver turned to Short Albino1 and continued animated discussions. The bodyguard walked off.

Martinez, Kyle behind him, saw the bodyguard conversing with Short Albino3 in a pink cap. He quickened his walking pace.

Short Albino3 saw him coming and smiled widely. The bodyguard returned a smile meant for Martinez.

“Can I help you?” Martinez asked.

The bodyguard turned and responded in a firmer, emphatic tone. “Can I HELP you?” He countered.

Martinez’s voice went up a couple of octaves. “Wha, wha, what—”

The driver, in conversation, heard voices getting louder, turned, and yelled, “Fellas, fellas, stop.”

He walked over, forced his way in between both men, and pushed them away from each other towards the middle of the room.

“Orosco, meet Martinez.”

Pointed to Martinez. “Martinez, meet Orosco, my new bodyguard.”

Martinez walked away towards Short Albino3.

“What’s the deal with that guy?” The bodyguard queried.

“He doesn’t like people talking to his workers, especially Short Albino3.”

“He got something going on with her?” The bodyguard asked.

“You jealous?”

"Hell, no. I'll poke through that short number with ease."

"You're sick,"

Orosco walked off with an attitude, mumbling.

Outside, all four Short Albinos loaded the truck in front of the shed. Martinez entered the truck and arranged the boxes as they were passed to him.

He beckoned Kyle to join. He jumped inside the truck.

Orosco sat beside the older man on the porch, both sipping liquor. "You own this place?"

"Are you stupid or just dumb?" The older man asked.

"Peaceful here, Pops," Orosco observed, waving empty hands across the old man's face to test if he was blind. No reaction.

"You do anything else, boy?" The older man asked. Orosco shrugged.

"I go to the gun range to practice."

"With the Mexican police?" The older man quipped and laughed.

Ridiculed, Orosco took a pistol from a shoulder harness, twirled like a cowboy, and almost dropped the gun.

He stared sheepishly at the older man to gauge whether he saw his awkward efforts. The older man remained expressionless.

"You know much about guns, son?"

"I know they shoot.

"They kill, too." The old timer elaborated and tuned him out.

"Martinez, your son? Orosco asked. No response. No movement.

"Hey, old-timer. You dead?" Orosco waved a hand back and forth in the older man's face.

"Take the fucking hand off my face before I shove it up your narrow ass."

Orosco jumped back. "Shit, old man, you are one sneaky bastard."

The loaded truck pulled up in front of the cottage. The driver got off, picked up a large brown envelope, and walked to the porch.

"Guadalupe in?" No response.

"Come on, old-timer. You know she, ma girl."

The older man turned to the driver and pointed to Orosco.

"He's gon get you killed, or more likely, accidentally kill you by himself."

"Why, you old goat—" The driver turned to Orosco.

"Get in the damn truck right now." Orosco hesitated.

The driver pointed at Orosco. "I ain't playing with you."

Orosco walked off the porch.

The driver handed the older man a brown envelope and walked off the porch. "I'll be seeing you."

"Drop dead," the old man replied. The truck drove off.

Guadalupe came out of the cottage onto the porch. The older man handed her the brown envelope.

She fished in the bag full of $100 bill bundles. "Pendejo," she said, looking at the truck.

While walking up from the factory, Martinez and Kyle watched the truck speed away. "Where's it going?"

Martinez turned to look at him. "That kind of question gets people killed around here."

"Really?"

Martinez busted out in laughter. "I'm just fucking with you. Selma."

"Where?" Kyle was confused.

"Selma, Alabama," Martinez repeated, staring at Kyle in a weird, dumb way.

Chapter 9

Up north in San Diego, the summer gradually turned hotter than was usual in the 'Mediterranean of the Americas.'

Billy Pearse had approached the condo HOA admin for approval to install a window air conditioner. His request was rejected because it would violate an HOA ordinance. Billy grudgingly accepted and invested in fans to cool himself down during the heat wave.

Now returning from his daily walk, he was hit in the face with a misty spray from an illegal window air conditioner condensate.

He was angry. "What the hell?" He said, wiping the mist from his eyes and looking up.

"That ain't right!" He said as he took out his cell phone and took pictures of the air conditioner.

The window on the other side of the air conditioner slid open, and eighteen-year-old Hudson Brenton stuck his head out.

"What the hell are you doing, old man? Taking pictures of my shit?"

Billy snapped more pictures and walked away.

Hudson stretched his head further and yelled, "Hey, I'm talking to you, old goat."

Billy turned a corner, and Hudson returned inside and closed the window.

Inside Hudson's Condo unit lounge, Derek Armstrong, his roommate of the same age, focused completely on a college football game on television while Hudson opened his mail.

Hudson yelled, "Stupid old goat. I'm going to kill him!"

"I'm watching TV here. Keep it the hell down," Derek sneered.

Hudson shoved the mail in Derek's face. "Look at this shit."

Derek did a quick scan, looked at Hudson in astonishment, and began to read the mail out loud:

"Dear Mister Brenton, For installing prohibited window air conditioning in direct violation of Rule 13 c, Section 7 of the HOA bylaws, you're hereby fined $1,500, payable within two weeks from the date of this letter.

"Delinquency adds a 10% surcharge every week until the principal sum is relieved. The HOA has filed a civil suit against you for:

(i) Property damage.

(ii) Passerby endangerment.

(iii) A court date subpoena is on the way.

Sincerely,

Janine Hawk,

HOA Administrator"

A week later, Hudson and Derek followed thirty yards behind Billy on the Condo sidewalk at night on an evening walk.

Derek admonished an eager Hudson. "Slow down, dude. He'll spot us." "Pussy!" Tyler disparaged.

Billy turned a corner to the darkest part of the walk route.

"This stretch is perfect," Hudson suggested.

They closed the gap with Billy, slipped on woolly face masks, and bookended Billy.

Seconds later, Hudson shoved Billy into the thorny brush. Billy fell into the bush, face-first.

"What the hell?" Billy grimaced, face down in the thorns.

Hudson rained down kicks, Billy curled up in pain and tried to protect himself, and Derek stood back. Hudson yelled at him. “Get in here, Derek, punk ass sissy bitch.” Derek did not move.

Hudson landed one more kick; Billy vomited. Crud flew out and splashed onto Hudson’s shoes. Billy passed out.

“Son of a bitch!” Hudson cursed and moved in again. Derek pulled him back. “You going to kill him? He’s old, man.” “Yeah. The old goat deserved it.”

Hudson, gasping, looked up to see a silhouette approaching. “I’m out of here,” he announced, running off. Derek followed suit.

At the Haka-Liki restaurant, a Maori-themed eatery, the fierceness of the Hiro temple on the wall-facing cellar steps shocked first-timers.

It was ten in the morning, and the red alarm light angled on the ceiling flashed and beeped to signal presence at the restaurant’s front door as Hayden worshipped at the Hiro temple.

He frowned at the wristwatch. It read 10:00 a.m. Restaurant doors opened at noon. He waited for the alarm to stop, but it didn’t.

Outside, Vlad Petroska, in his late twenties, kept his finger on the doorbell. His cousin, Kilick Novotnik, a year older, was beside him.

Hayden appeared behind the door. Fear flashed across his eyes once he saw the Ukrainians. "Oh... shit!"

He unlocked and opened the door to let the cousins inside, then locked it behind them. Vlad and Kilick chose a corner table.

Hayden walked behind the bar table and switched on all the lights and CCTVs. Fierce Māori war dances looped on the video playing.

Vlad stared hard at Hayden, making a drinking motion with his hand. Hayden brought hard liquor and glasses.

Vlad invited him to join. He begged off. Kilick grabbed Hayden's wrist. "You got the 200-large Kiwi boy?" "I need more—"

Kilick snapped Hayden's wrist, breaking it.

Hayden screamed, cradled his broken wrist, crouched, and walked away. The Ukrainians burst out in laughter as they walked out of the restaurant.

Colt Brenton looped a white mesh bag over his head and slung it across his left shoulder when he got to Del Mar beach.

He picked up a white surfboard from the sand, walked into the ocean, and paddled out to sea.

Hayden Brenton, right arm encased in a white cast from his wrist to his elbow, rushed into the sea with a surfboard, going after his brother Colt.

Colt looked back to see Hayden in pursuit, and he paddled faster. Hayden drifted further back from Colt and yelled in frustration, "Goddamnit, Colt, don't throw Hiro away, you stupid shit."

Hayden stopped paddling, exhausted and frustrated. He watched Colt get farther and farther out to sea.

A sudden gigantic whoosh from below the water's surface flung the surfboard up in the air, along with Colt. A large whale with its tail slapped Colt and the surfboard hundreds of yards farther into the ocean and then submerged.

Hayden froze in place, mouth agape. He soon recovered and started to yell, "What the shit... What the shit..."

A white mesh bag popped up next to Hayden, and he jumped in fright. "Bastard!"

He fished out the bag, extracted the Hiro mask, held the mask dearly to his chest, and hurried ashore.

An hour later, Hayden, with the mesh bag across his shoulder, stood beside a Cop, answering questions amid flashing patrol cars.

The Cop asked, “What’s in the bag?”

“Hiro.”

“What?”

“Māori mask.”

“Anyway, what’s it doing here?”

“Popped up after Colt got thrown.”

The Cop suspiciously stared at Hayden.

“It’s evidence.”

“How can it possibly be?” Hayden wanted to know.

“So, you’re sticking with your story? A large whale threw your brother?”

The Cop sneered at Hayden’s wrist cast. Hayden followed his eyes.

“Did you two fight?”

“Oh, no, no, no. I fell and broke my wrist.”

“When was the last time you saw your brother?”

Hayden hesitated. The Cop stepped in closer, and Hayden reared back.

“Well, we fought. We had a verbal altercation this morning, but no physical stuff.”

The Cop’s face hardened.

“...and you decided to drown him, right?”

The Cop continued, “You know his body will eventually pop up. They always do!”

“I need to get out of here. Are you accusing me of killing my brother while I’m trying to figure out a way to tell his son?”

Hayden began to walk away, and the Cop raised his voice, “If you do not explain what happened between you and your brother this morning, I’ll have you arrested for homicide.”

Hayden stopped, looked at the Cop incredulously, and returned to him.

“Are you shitting me? I lost my brother, and you accuse me of murder?”

The Cop reached for handcuffs.

“Really?” Hayden could not believe it.

“Yeah. Hands behind your back.”

“Okay, okay. I’ll tell you what happened...”

Colt, fuming, stormed out of the receiving dock behind the restaurant, Hayden following.

Colt turned and pointed a finger. “Stay away from Hudson. He’s my son, not yours.”

"You're clueless and have no idea how great a young man Hudson is becoming."

Colt snickered. "Yeah. We're back to your perennial excuse to usurp my son again."

Hayden's head hung in sorrow.

"I'm so sorry."

He walked away.

Colt ran after him in confrontation.

"You should settle your damn gambling debts with those fucking Russians and let me worry about my son."

"Ukrainians, and it's none of your concerns."

Hayden walked away again. Colt wouldn't let go. He got in his face again.

"I plan to get rid of Hiro. It's time you drown the deaf, dumb, and lifeless wooden motherfucker."

Hayden went ballistic. He got into Colt's face. Colt reared back in shock.

"You touch Hiro, I'll kill you."

He walked away emphatically, opened the restaurant's back door, and went inside.

Colt fumed and paced angrily.

"... Brothers having a tiff," Hayden concluded.

"You have a cast on your arm. You told me you fought this morning over a mask; you have it around your neck. Now your brother has disappeared."

"I know it doesn't look good, but it's what happened."

The Cop studied him for a long while.

"I will let you go for now, but expect detective visits. God will help you if your brother floats back up."

Hayden walked away in sadness, talking to himself. "How the hell do I tell Hudson?"

The following day, at the Home Depot, Billy, with a wounded face, carefully slid out of the SUV.

"What's the fastest-drying, clear glue you carry?"

Customer service personnel punched keys on the computer and looked up.

"Basic or professional use?"

"Same difference, right?"

The customer service member's face lit up. "Glue is really for routine home use. Adhesives, on the other hand, are professional and cost more."

"Which is stickier?"

"Depends upon—"

"What aisle?" Billy was impatient.

The store clerk deflated in enthusiasm.

"Fifteen, sir," and he walked away before Billy uttered another word.

"Punk," Billy muttered as he went.

He picked items up in aisle fifteen and checked out.

Billy broke into Hudson's condo the next morning and shuddered when he saw a temple.

"Ay ay ay... holy shit."

A fierce Hiro mask hung in the middle of the wall, immediately below a mantle that held several burning mini-red candles within the large molten wax mound.

He stopped to gaze briefly and hesitated with second thoughts. "Gives me the willies. Uh!"

He walked farther, wrinkling his nose, when he came near the glass center table with an overflowing ashtray beside a dirty mug. "Filthy pigs."

He pulled down the toilet bowl seat in the bathroom, dabbed rubbing alcohol on a towel, wiped the seat clean, thinly spread adhesive onto the seat, and blow-dried it.

He walked into the bedroom, saw Derek's picture on a dresser, and walked right back out.

In the next bedroom, he saw a portrait of Hudson on a dresser. He pulled out drawers until he found boxer shorts. He pulled out six.

He turned the shorts inside out on the bed, applied adhesives, blow-dried them, and returned them to the drawer. He walked towards the door to leave.

With his hand on the door handle, he heard keys turn in the lock, but it was too close for Billy to run.

Hudson walked in, saw Billy, and kicked the door shut with the back of his heel. "What the fuck?"

He tackled Billy and immediately forced him back into the unit.

The center table toppled, cracking the glass. Mugs and ashtrays went flying.

Billy was no match but held on as Hudson pushed him away to create space between them. He punched Billy in the back.

Billy held on tight, and they both bumped into the temple wall. Hudson saw the mantle, candles, and mask wobble.

"Oh shit, oh shit," he lamented amidst the grapple.

Hudson maneuvered them away from the temple, and Billy pushed them further into the temple.

The temple toppled and began to fall, and a huge blob of hot wax deposited on Billy's left wrist. He winced and yelled in pain. "Goddamn idol shit, ass."

Hudson let go of Billy to catch the mask as it fell from the wall. Billy let go of Hudson and grabbed his left wrist.

Hudson caught the mask before it hit the floor with much relief. Billy, blowing on his burnt wrist, watched Hudson curiously.

"I'm calling the Cops," Hudson announced. Billy reached out, grabbed a mug, and whacked Hudson on the head.

"What the..." The mask fell out of Hudson's hands onto the floor as he slumped and passed out.

Billy passed out at the same time the mask touched the floor.

Moments later, Billy woke up, grabbed his swollen left wrist, now with a nasty burn, looked up, and saw Hudson still out. The mask sat perfectly on his face.

"Weirdos," Billy said and bolted from the unit.

Ten minutes later, Hudson woke up.

"Oh, this isn't good; it's very bad," he repeated as he repaired the temple.

Chapter 10

It was nighttime at Billy's lounge.

Billy massaged his bandaged, burned wrist and listened to his voicemail as he watched muted TV. He skipped several messages until he got to Kyle's.

"Sylvia ain't too happy with you. You've got to call her. Me? I don't care because I know you, but call her."

Billy shut the phone down after the message ended and stared at the TV screen expressionlessly.

A sudden older version of Jordan's face appeared on the TV screen as Billy watched the news in his condo lounge, feverishly scratching the nasty burn from the Maori temple scuffle. He jumped in fright.

Jordan spoke, "Your guilt has registered after decades of abandonment of your siblings. It's time to move on."

Billy tried to speak and move. He couldn't.

"Kyle is strong and never gives up, but the weight of responsibilities has scarred him," Jordan stated.

Billy tried to speak again, but couldn't.

"Sylvia is barely holding on to sanity. Once, she was a pole dancer who tried to adopt unsuccessfully and had no life prospects. She's now trapped with someone crooked.

Big brothers are supposed to support and console their younger siblings. You haven't done either, Billy."

A single tear dropped from Billy's left eye.

The TV screen turned black and white, showing Sylvia at home...

Alonzo angrily addressed Sylvia, standing in her face.

"You never respect me, no matter what I do."

Sylvia grabbed hold of his shirt as he walked away. He tried to free himself.

"You need to give respect to get r-e-s-p-e-c-t."

Alonzo turned in anger and slugged Sylvia in the face. She dropped to the floor hard.

Alonzo sat on the sofa and stared at Sylvia on the floor, unmoving.

He stood up, walked into the kitchen, returned with a cup of water, and splashed it over Sylvia's face. She jerked up.

Her face was cut and bleeding, and her left eye was black and blue, swollen shut.

"See what you made me do?" Alonzo lamented.

Sylvia sat up and moved her jaw to test if it was broken. She felt her face and winced in pain. Struggling to get up, she eventually walked to the kitchen.

Alonzo stood up, dialed his cell phone, and turned his back to the kitchen.

Sylvia entered the lounge and plunged a long stainless-steel knife into Alonzo's back.

"No one lays a hand on me, motherfucker!"

Alonzo screamed in pain. Blood oozed through the shirt. He tried to pull the knife out.

Sylvia fished in her pocket as she ran outside. She dialed 911.

"I think I've killed my boyfriend!"

"Slow down, miss, and tell me where you are," the emergency responder asked.

"Motherfucker punched me, so I stabbed him."

The operator interrupted, "Tell me where you are, miss. Things are not as bad as they seem."

"I'm at..."

She went back inside.

Alonzo lay on the floor, not moving. The siren sounds got louder.

Sylvia was on the sofa and started to cry. She slid off onto the floor, unconscious.

Alonzo survived the ordeal...

Billy also passed out, scratching his wound.

***

Father Joe smiled as Billy walked in late in the evening. "We have a new produce buyer to support you."

"Did Garcia blow up the kitchen?"

Father Joe waved his hands for Billy to stop. "We all have our roles to play, son. You've given your time and soul to this place for years, and we're all not getting any younger."

Billy sighed in surrender. "I accept. Is he here?"

"Yes, and he's a she. Waiting in the kitchen."

Billy hurried out. Father Joe smiled knowingly.

Billy walked into the kitchen and saw the forty-five-year-old Carmen Soto from behind, talking to Garcia and cooking.

Garcia's eyes shifted to Billy, and Carmen turned to look. Billy was immediately smitten.

She glided to him with a warm, wide smile and thrust out a hand for a handshake. "I'm Carmen Soto, your produce buyer."

Billy remained mute for a few seconds, then shook the extended hand.

"Would you like to talk in my new office?" she asked, didn't wait for an answer, and headed out of the kitchen.

Billy locked eyes with Garcia, who gestured and mouthed, Go, go.

In her office, Carmen asked, "You're not threatened by my presence here, are you?"

Billy masked his surprise at her directness with a smile. "I'm glad you're letting me get a word in."

She laughed out loud and touched his arm, enjoying the laughter. "Don't mind me, mister Pearse. I meant no harm. I'm privileged to work here. As an RN, I come across sad stories. So, when can I laugh?" She trailed off.

"Will you have dinner with me?" Billy asked.

"What?"

He chuckled to hide his discomfort. "I don't know why I blurted that out."

He got up, ready to bolt, but Carmen's voice stopped him. "Why don't you wait to see if I can pick the best zucchini, find the freshest lettuce, and bring in the sweetest carrots? If you still haven't changed your mind, I'll think about it."

He stopped by the door, looked back, smiled, then left.

A month later, Billy and Carmen were dating.

Carmen and Billy were at the dining table finishing a meal.

“Did you enjoy it? Is it true it’s hard to cook for a cook?” she asked.

“Much like performing surgery on a doctor.”

Carmen took a long look at him and smiled seductively. “Coffee? Doctor Cook?”

Billy moved to the sofa to watch TV.

Carmen arrived with steaming mugs. She cozied up to him, and they linked arms.

***

Hudson walked sluggishly into the bathroom mid-morning. He looked at himself in the mirror. His eyes were bloodshot.

He spat blood into the sink, and a molar fell out, then rolled and disappeared down the sinkhole.

He stepped closer to the mirror, opened his mouth wide to inspect the molar cavity, stepped back, murmured, “Fucking old goat,” and walked back into the lounge.

The temple was all over the floor.

His curiosity piqued as he repaired it.

By mid-afternoon, Derek was perched on the toilet bowl, playing music on his cell phone. He rolled the joint, fired the joint, smoked the joint, and grunted to expel a hard dump.

He pulled toilet roll sheets, but his ass cheek was stuck to the toilet seat. “What the hell?” he said.

He tried again and again.

“What the fuck is going on here?” he grunted louder. He tried to get up, pulling harder.

He yelled in pain as blood spots appeared between his ass cheek and the toilet bowl seat.

He grabbed the cell phone and dialed. “My ass is stuck to the toilet bowl seat.”

Hudson cackled. “You’re shitting me?” He laughed even harder at the irony of his response.

Derek yelled, “This is not fucking funny. I think your idol shit is fucking with me. It’s all over the floor.”

“Again?” Hudson asked and then continued, “Okay, I’m there. Don’t go anywhere.” He laughed again at his new irony.

“Asshole,” Derek concluded before cutting the line in anger.

Emergency responders unscrewed the toilet bowl seat and carried Derek out on a stretcher.

At the door, Derek blew up in anger at Hudson, "You and your fucking idol shit!"

It's morning at the Haka-Liki restaurant. Hayden and Hudson nursed their coffee but were not ready to open the restaurant.

"Temple kept falling to the floor each time I repaired it, man! Can you help?"

"Yes and no. I can advise you on what needs to be done, but you must do it yourself. Tradition calls for retaliation against whoever caused it to touch the floor first."

Hudson jumped off the chair. "Then I'm killing the old goat—"

"Taking a life isn't easy, nor something to trifle with. I've heard of a ritual to replace forfeiture of life, but have you called in favors from old masters in New Zealand?"

"I don't have time, Uncle Hayden. I'm falling apart here. My tooth, my eyes, Jesus! What do I do in the meantime?"

Hayden shifted uncomfortably at the word "Jesus."

"Keep repairing the temple and stay the fuck away from the 'old goat.'"

Hudson murmured something unintelligible.

"What?"

"Nothing!"

"I love you, kid. I'll never steer you wrong. You're the only family I have left. Just stay away from the old guy."

"Okay, okay."

Billy was in bed watching TV when he dozed off. Soon, he jerked in a fitful nightmare...

He was on a balcony, his hands spread wide on the railing, watching his youngest sibling, Jordan, fall backward. Jordan looked up at Billy as he fell, pleading for help.

Billy first snickered and then burst out in full hysterical laughter.

...Billy woke up and jumped off the bed, sweating. White TV noise freaked him out even more. He gasped for air.

He sat down, grabbed his cell phone, and called Carmen.

Carmen, saddened by worries, peered through the curtained window. She saw a car pull up, and Billy stepped out.

"It's 2:00 am, Billy? You scared me to death."

He pecked her on the cheek and walked past her towards the bedroom.

He pulled off his jacket, wearing his pajamas underneath. He sat on the bed.

She pointed at him. “Did you drive in your PJs?”

“What?” He looked at himself and tugged at his clothes. “Oh, shit.”

Carmen sat very close to him and caressed his arm. He broke down, eyes streaming with tears.

Carmen pleaded lovingly. “How can I help?”

Billy released a huge sigh.

“I graduated from college at twenty-four and celebrated with my best friend when my mom was at work.”

He took in a deep breath.

“I sent my brothers, Kyle and Jordan, along with my sister, Sylvia, to the bedroom. They were fourteen, nine, and five at the time.”

Billy held his head in his hands and whimpered. Carmen pacified him.

“I’m here, Billy.”

“My best friend and I got drunk and nodded off on the sofa. Jordan came out of the room while we were out cold... went onto the balcony...”

Billy took another huge breath.

“Long story short, Jordan, at five, fell off the third-floor balcony.”

Carmen gripped his arm harder, about to start crying. He was now soothing her.

“It gets worse, Carmen...”

She looked up with a questioning stare.

“Before Jordan fell, my mother, Florence, was in the parking lot below, returning from her second job. She saw Jordan fall and rushed to him. Suffered a heart attack, collapsed, and died right there and then, next to her youngest child.”

Carmen burst out crying. Billy consoled her. In a sad embrace, they both lay down on the bed.

Moments later, Carmen spoke in a quiet, loving, but firm voice, “You know what you must now do, starting with Hudson.”

He did not speak, but he held her tighter instead.

Billy knocked on Hudson's door. Hudson looked through the peephole and saw Billy. He reared back as if pulled from behind.

"I can hear you moving in there, Hudson, and I'm not leaving anytime soon until you open the door."

Hudson stood perplexed and indecisive. He soon relented, cracked the door open, and scowled.

"What the hell do you want?"

"Please, let me in," Billy pleaded.

"Not until you tell me what you want."

"I'm here to apologize."

Stunned in confusion, Hudson didn't know what to do for a few seconds.

"What?"

"I want to apologize for..." Hudson let him in before he could finish.

Billy sat on the sofa by the center table with the cracked glass.

"...for all the heartache I must have caused you, and—"

"You mean like my molar falling out?"

He opened his mouth wide to show Billy.

"Look at me. I'm like the fucking Dracula. Sunken eyes, no energy. You fucked me up, you old goat."

He then followed with streams of expletives until he wore himself out and collapsed on the sofa across the center table from Billy.

"I'm sorry, Hudson. Please accept my apologies. I had no idea what the HOA would do."

Hudson was receptive to the apology until Billy saw a glossy flyer picture on the center table. The picture announced a first-anniversary discount at Haka-Liki restaurant.

Billy picked up the flyer. Hudson snatched it off him immediately.

"Don't touch it."

"I know the restaurant and the guy in the picture," Billy confessed.

"He's my father... You don't know him. I need you to leave now."

"What happened to him?"

Hudson got up in Billy's face and urged him to leave.

"All right. I got it. But I need to know if you and I are okay here."

Hudson stepped back a little and gave an insincere, noncommittal nod.

"Yeah, yeah, yeah, we're okay. Get the fuck out right now."

Billy left unfulfilled.

Chapter 11

Pale as a ghost, Hudson walked into the lounge in the morning and saw the temple on the floor again. With low energy, he repaired the temple and headed for the bathroom.

He turned the shower on and pulled off his boxer shorts. They didn't come off. He stood, confused, for a few seconds and tried again without success. Then, he gradually got angry.

"Fucking old goat. I'm going to kill him. Apologize, my ass."

He stepped into the shower with his boxer shorts, cursing.

It was evening now as he knocked on Billy's door.

Billy beamed when he saw him through the peephole. He opened the door wide, and Hudson stepped inside.

He halted in surprise when he saw Carmen on the sofa and hesitated to proceed.

He went inside and sat on the sofa across the center table from Billy and Carmen.

Billy introduced Carmen. "This is Carmen."

Carmen smiled warmly at Hudson.

Mad and unhappy, Hudson put on a pasty smile and got right into it with Billy.

"Why did you try so hard to destroy me?"

"I'm so sorry for all the harm I caused you."

Hudson interrupted, "Apologies aside. Why not stop once you'd reported the air conditioner? Did you have to glue everything up?"

"Reasons and whys don't matter now, Hudson. I need to move on. Please, help me."

Hudson calmed down, and Billy continued. "I know the man I saw in the flyer at your place. Colt Brenton. He and—"

Hudson exploded and stood over Billy threateningly. Billy remained seated passively.

Hudson then walked towards the front door. He stopped when Carmen started talking. "Please, listen to me for a minute."

Hudson stared at her, and she continued.

"Billy lost both his five-year-old brother and forty-year-old mother on the same day.

"His brother fell from a third-floor window balcony, and his mother witnessed the fall.

"She collapsed with a heart attack and died on the spot.

"Billy was not much older than you are now."

Hudson stared at Billy for a long time as his tough facade gradually crumbled. He returned to squeeze in between Carmen and Billy on the two-seater sofa.

Carmen continued, "Billy had not spoken to his living relatives, Kyle and Sylvia, for over three decades. I'm not making excuses for him..."

Hudson raised his hand for her to stop, reaching under his shirt and casually bringing out a long stainless-steel knife.

He laid it on the center table, slumped back on the sofa, and reclined his head on the backrest.

"I meant to stab Billy the moment he opened the door, not expecting anyone else to be present," Hudson confessed.

Billy and Carmen sat forward on the sofa, captivated by the gleaming blade for a long time.

"It would cause a lot of damage," Billy offered.

Moments later, Carmen and Hudson hugged awkwardly at the door.

Billy pulled Hudson to the side. “You have my open dinner invite whenever you wish, Hudson, but I’ll come to pick you up for lunch.”

Hudson walked off without a response to the invitation.

Minutes later, Hudson walked back into his condo lounge in high spirits, saw the temple on the floor, and ignored it.

He collapsed on the sofa with a faraway, pleasant look and yelled, “Come out here, Derek.”

Nothing happened for longer than normal. Hudson got up and walked into Derek’s room. It was completely bare.

Hudson slumped emotionally. He flopped on Derek’s bare bed. “Shit.”

Billy knocked on Hudson’s door the following morning.

When the door opened, Billy walked in, ignored the temple on the floor, and noticed Hudson's despondency.

“Is everything okay?”

Hudson sat down across the table from Billy.

“It’s nothing.”

“Are you psyched up for lunch?”

Hudson looked him over curiously. “What?”

"Lunch with me, man!" Billy said, smiling.

"Yeah!" Hudson's answer was laden with sarcasm.

"I feel something's wrong."

Hudson hurried them out of the unit, saddened by the loss of his friend, Derek, who had moved out.

It was afternoon when Billy and Hudson walked down the street toward Father Joe's soup kitchen.

Father Joe waved them over as they hit the dining hall. Hudson stared at Billy questioningly.

"The Father is expecting us," Billy said calmly.

Hudson brooded as they sat on either side of Father Joe, who was at the table's head.

"What am I doing here?"

"Lunch, as promised." Billy offered.

Steaming Styrofoam food plates arrived.

"Billy has told me all about you and his role in your life. I first met Billy more than twenty-five years ago."

Hudson shrugged and looked at Billy suspiciously.

"Billy has missed only one or two volunteering days here for fifteen years."

Hudson now stared at Billy with a softer, curious look as Billy ate.

"Please, dig in. I promise you'll enjoy the meal. We have a young man in the back, Garcia Lopez, the same age as you, who does wonders."

All three ate in silence. Hudson looked up in pleasant surprise at Father Joe.

"The food's very good," he said. Father Joe smiled.

"Did you know Carmen also volunteers here?"

Hudson frowned. "I thought she was an RN?"

"She is, but she's also our produce buyer."

Hudson stopped eating and dropped his cutlery. "Okay, guys. Is this an intervention?"

Billy smiled. "Not at all. It's the best place I know where the food is perfect, and chatting with Father Joe is always soothing, especially when I'm troubled." Billy's voice trailed off.

"Hudson, I never preach to anyone, but you'll be welcome to volunteer here if you'd like."

Father Joe got up. "Well, it's been nice meeting you, Hudson. Hope we see more of you here shortly."

Father Joe walked away, and Hudson eyeballed Billy. "I know you planned this."

Billy smiled. “I wanted you to see me in a better light beyond the worst parts of me you’ve seen thus far.”

Hudson waved him off. “All right, all right, this is getting too soapy. I forgive you. Can we leave now?”

They both walked out of the soup kitchen.

Inside Hudson’s Condo lounge, the temple was all over the floor again.

Hudson smoked weed while watching TV. His phone rang.

He answered, then sat up straighter in utter fright. He rushed out of the condo.

Inside Haka-Liki, a white sheet covered Hayden’s body on the floor. His left shoe stuck out.

The emergency response team (ERT) buzzed the body. Police questioned Hudson at the bar.

“The victim is your uncle?”

“Why would anyone want to kill him?” Hudson asked.

“How old are you, son?”

“Do you know who killed him?”

“When was the last time you saw him?

“A week ago. Who killed my uncle?”

“Do you have anyone older in your family you can call?”

“Why? I’m eighteen, and he was my uncle.”

Hudson bent down low as if hit by something. A Cop nearby signaled ERT personnel to approach.

The Cop walked away, and an older ERT person stepped toward Hudson.

“I’m okay. I felt queasy. I don’t know why.”

“It’s a delayed shock reaction, son. Do you have anyone you can call?”

“What do you mean?”

“Emotional trauma can wreak havoc on your psyche, so any support you can get from family and close friends will help.”

Hudson teared up.

“Hey, hey, try and hold it together, son.”

He made Hudson stand upright for a few seconds, then sit on the bar stool, both feet on the bar footrest.

He gave him a glass of water. Hudson emptied the glass in a single gulp. “Slow down, son.”

Hudson coughed.

"Want me to call somebody for you?"

Hudson replied weakly, "No." He brought out his cell phone and pretended to dial. ERT personnel walked away. Hudson's head dropped in sadness, but he made a call anyway.

It was evening now, and the Haka-Liki restaurant's front door opened. Carmen and Billy walked in.

Hudson glided towards her, who openly received him into her arms. Billy hung back, watching them both whimper quietly.

Chapter 12

Three young men, full of self-confidence, strolled down a Texas avenue. They busted out in an acapella of a Betty Carter song, "Ain't Nothin' But Soul. All three were senior A students in music with a minor in political science at the Art Institute of Houston.

Hearing them sing was incongruent with how they looked and dressed for anyone watching from afar, but not those hearing the blended, amazing, harmonized voices.

The tallest of the trio had tats all over his exposed arms and neck; the second, of medium height, was almost bald except for a tuft of hair on his temple; and the third was weird-looking, with a tangled Rastafari hairdo and glasses that contrasted sharply with his persona.

Just as they started singing, they stopped in front of a small office in downtown Houston, the Palmer Recording Studios on Lyons Avenue.

Palmer, the studio owner, waited for the three young men to settle down inside the recording cordon. When ready, he hand-signaled them to start. The tallest tattooed singer spoke, "We're ready to blow up this here muterfucking rhythm."

Palmer immediately shut everything down and waved them outside the recording cordon to his side in the control room. He allowed them to simmer again as they crowded each other on the couch before him.

"Listen, kids, what are you looking for?"

"Muterfucking rhythms," the same tall guy repeated with more enthusiasm.

Palmer glared. They all stood up. "Listen, kids, your voice teacher, Alcindo, was my classmate long ago. He recommended I listen to you, thinking you have talent." All three smiled with confidence. Palmer then pulled closer to them.

"Now, listen and listen real good. When you're here, we speak normally and treat each other with respect and dignity, which I know you all possess. Now, I ask you again, what exactly are you looking for?"

The same tall guy responded, "The opportunity to present our talent for all to appreciate…"

The weird-looking Rastafari interrupted, "While treating the environment as it should…"

The third, almost bald guy, then concluded. "We're all Gen Z; we don't want money or too much fame, but we want to live a full life with minimum environmental damage."

The room went quiet but for the low hum of the heavy electronics. Then Palmer smiled, and everyone relaxed.

“Goddamn. I love it. Now, get back inside and show me what y’all got.”

The kids rushed back into the recording cordon as Palmer slid, turned, and tweaked the recording panel, ready to be dazzled. Five minutes later, he lay back, dazzled.

An hour later, they all sat down, relaxed, in the control room, sipping liquor. Palmer spoke, “I have a suggestion and a proposal…” He allowed his words to linger. The boys sat forward.

“To get you on the musical map, you will become ambassadors for revitalizing an abandoned warehouse in a neglected section of Houston to establish your brand.

“I will engage a contractor to look for a property we can promote, touting your environmental proclivity…”

Palmer looked around. A chorus of “yes, yes, yes” followed.

Thirty minutes later, the kids filed out, belting out an Acapella, as Palmer sat back, watched, and smiled.

The contractor walked Palmer into an abandoned warehouse in the Houston 5th Ward, the cultural arts district.

Palmer looked around in disgust. “This is pretty dismal. Not exactly what I was looking for.”

The contractor smiled. “For a creative guy, you’re not looking beyond possibilities here.”

Palmer chuckled. “I hate to be obvious, but slapping lipstick on a pig doesn’t exactly make you Taylor Swift. Right?”

“JLo will emerge when the makeup has been applied, and the face is buffed and blow-dried,” the contractor boasted.

Palmer shook his head in disbelief. “All these metaphors are unbecoming, man!”

“You started it.”

They kept walking, inspecting nooks and crevices as Palmer’s demeanor continued to dive until they reached a small brook with a fountain in the middle. The brackish water was uninviting.

Palmer, behind the contractor, stopped walking while the contractor kept talking to the air. Then, he sensed something off when there was no response to an innocuous statement. He turned around and walked back to Palmer, studying the murky water.

“What?” the contractor asked.

“We may have something here. My clients are Gen Z environmental bleeding hearts,” Palmer stated.

The contractor wrinkled his nose from the stench. “Now, that’s a pigsty, don’t you think?”

Palmer swung around. “Shouldn’t you be selling me on this?” Palmer accused.

The contractor laughed. Then, Palmer realized he was goading him.

“Real funny,” Palmer retorted and continued.

“I can see the kids getting a kick out of an office with a fountain in front of it.”

“Are you sold on this, Palmer?”

“Numbers?”

“Well...” the contractor stated as he crunched numbers on his cell phone. “It’d set you back a few pesos, amigo.”

“How long before it can look decent?” Palmer asked.

“You’re not worried about costs?”

“I can always say no if you...” Palmer hesitated and continued, “...if you misquote.”

The contractor laughed. “Give me a month to prod the local council for possible liens and approvals.”

Palmer smiled with an obvious guile. “Even for the 5th Ward, where the council should be glad of any interest and provide incentives?”

“Yeah. Where have you been? This is Texas, my friend.”

“Oh?” Palmer challenged.

"Hidden figures, man!"

"What?" Palmer was confused.

"There are noises of football teams looking."

Palmer poopooed it. "You wouldn't be trying to up-sell me, would you?"

"Who? Me?" The contractor faked shock.

Palmer began walking off the property, and the contractor hurried to follow.

The contractor gathered his plans for the site, along with the project summary, which included the history of the 5th Ward in the 18th congressional district of Harris County, Texas.

His team navigated the convoluted, multifaceted approval processes in the various governmental alphabet soup of departments.

Economic development impact calculations group, the perceived need for area revitalization entity, urban design, beautification association, employment by industry and occupation leadership, and building and permit data repository, to mention just a few.

They broke ground, so to speak, after three weeks.

At the site, a collection of heavy construction equipment tore down dilapidated structures beyond salvage and leveled those that were unnecessary. The first day went as expected.

The day offered great photo ops for Palmer and his three young tutelages as they watched the contractor and his team direct traffic amid the busy yet organized chaos.

"That's what I'm talking about," the tall kid addressed no one in particular when a heavy piece of equipment lopped off a section of the building.

The other two kids were busy taking pictures with a professional photographer from Palmer.

Palmer corralled the rambunctious, tall fellow. "Hey, get over here; it's unsafe to go beyond the roped-off area…" The kid ran back, still in awe of the whole process.

Then, day two threw everything into a tizzy when the fountain pond draining excavated three drums, which, when opened, scared the living daylight out of the laborers as human bones spilled out—those three bank robbers, Trevor Russo, Les Smith, and Dave Pelt, Kyle Pearse partnered with.

Work stoppage ensued immediately.

The Houston Skeletal Recovery Team (SRT), consisting of Forensic Anthropologists and Forensic Investigators, descended with fury at the morbid site, mindful of the recent bruhaha of their past lackadaisical attitude towards the "Artiste" types, tinging on being discriminatory.

Medical examiner services, the skeletal recovery and analysis department, forensic anthropologists, and personnel from the Identification Unit (ID Unit) were spread out at the work site.

The mayor laid out the objective at a press conference...

"We plan to recover and isolate the skeletal remains, develop profiles, analyze bone traumas, engender pathologies, and taphonomy activities sensitive to environmental organic remains passing to the lithosphere.

"The ID Unit will work with law enforcement to identify the remains by deploying DNA, fingerprint, dental X-ray, and other methodologies."

The Medical Examiner, ME, drooled with a deep Texas twang, captured by an overhead microphone recording the proceedings as he examined each of the three remains.

The ME lamented. "These are young bones. Though fully developed, they still seem young. Lives wasted," the ME concluded.

"Sadly," the assistant concurred as the ME continued.

“The first appears to be that of a well-developed, well-nourished Caucasian male. The bone weighed 10 pounds due to porosity caused by submersion seepage. Three bullet holes/apertures in the sternum, hip, and back of the head...”

The ME turned to his assistant to move the subject out and bring in the next one.

Within five hours, he had concluded his autopsy, and a detailed report was filed.

At his office, he sat with his assistant, both now in shirts and ties, to discuss what they knew would happen next and to be prepared for it.

“Sir, you don’t think they will assign Rory to this case, do you?”

“Never. It’s too big for Rory. Besides, he only has months to retire.”

The assistant shook his head in disagreement. “I don’t know about that. He grew up in the 5th Ward.”

The ME looked up from his writing. “What’s that got to do with anything?”

“Street code.”

“What are you, in a gang?” the ME challenged.

"No. I'm only saying Rory may want to prove something to himself."

"Like what?"

In exasperation, the assistant answered and got up to leave. "You always take care of your own."

"I thought he was Mexican?" the ME ridiculed, drawing the ire of his subordinate, who turned around by the door, hand on the doorknob.

"He's from Honduras. But like those three dead white boys yet to be identified, whatever else we may think, their last resting place was at that construction site in the 5th Ward, where Detective Rory Franco grew up."

The assistant left before the ME could respond.

Detective Rory Franco, sixty, rolled out of bed and reached for an old beat-up Bulova wristwatch by his bedside stand. It was smack at 6:00 a.m. His internal clock had won again.

He smiled and pulled himself out of his single-mattress bed, which his mother named 'El Ladrillo.'

Fully dressed in a suit, he yelled in a muted voice from the kitchen with a nice fried onion-filled aroma, "Te quieres desuyano, mama?"

His eighty-year-old mother, in her wheelchair, was already at the kitchen door, smiling.

“Tortillas, mi hijo.”

“Perfecto, mama,” he said without looking.

“Gracias.” She settled at the large dining table as Rory laid out the perfectly fried soft omelet for her, garnished with parsley.

His mother looked up just before she began eating. “Y tu?”

“Nada, mamá. Solo café, gracias,” Rory said as he kissed her head and headed out of their Frenchtown home in the Houston 5th Ward they’d lived in since he was a lad.

He walked down the street, acknowledging neighbors as he got into his old Volvo parked on the street.

He strolled into the Downtown Houston police precinct and headed for the small kitchen for his habitual second cup of coffee to start his day.

On the way to his cubicle, he back-slapped a few colleagues, mostly younger than he was. A voice called out to him. “Got a minute?”

Rory turned around to see his Chief beckoning him over.

The Chief sat him down with a wary look. "You up for a job?"

Rory frowned. "Two months and counting, jefe."

"Si. Pero yo tengo un trabajo interesante para ti."

"No, gracias, jefe." Rory got up.

"Don't you even want to know what it is?" his boss asked.

"No. Two months and counting." Rory approached the door to exit.

"Even if it's on the 5th Ward?"

Rory stopped, turned around, and looked at his boss curiously. His boss continued. "Let me show you something."

Rory's boss led the way to a conference room.

Inside, a projector showed a blank white screen until a series of still pictures appeared when it was turned on.

Rory turned to face his younger boss. "So?"

These are summary stills from an SRT investigation of three remains recovered from an abandoned warehouse under reclamation. And knowing your ties to the area, I thought of you."

Rory's guided interest became obvious, but he was not yet convinced. "What's the story, and why us?"

"It so happened that only one of the bodies could be positively identified. I want you to find out if he has any relatives."

"Anyone can do that," Rory shot back.

"But this is the 5th Ward, your home. Ain't you curious?"

"No. I just want to put in my time, do my crosswords, drink coffee, and not get shot just before I cash in."

"I'll tell you what, Rory, give it two weeks, and if nothing shows, I'll reassign the case."

Rory stared hard at his boss. "You know how hard it is to transition investigations, so, no."

"What if I assign you a partner right now?"

Rory got out of his chair in protest. "Oh, hell, no."

"That's what I thought. Either you get a partner, do it independently, or I will fiddle with your retirement dates."

Rory got into his boss's face. "Is that a threat?"

"Damn right." The Chief then pointed to a side table with a pile of files. "You'll find all you need in there," he said and walked out, leaving Rory angry and frustrated.

After simmering in his anger for several minutes, he started flipping through the files.

It was well known and understood across the Houston police precinct that desk-bound, take-no-risks, near-retirement detective Rory Franco was looking forward to retiring in his native Honduras town and had sworn off any risky assignment that could turn dangerous at the last minute.

Chapter 13

Detective Rory Franco arrived at the warehouse less enthusiastic. He walked around expertly, taking in the sights.

The fountain with its brackish water loomed large, all roped off and sequestered.

He bent down low, looking at a dirty pool with all kinds of scum floating. He stood up and walked towards the warehouse, half-torn down. He sighted old tire marks leading to the entrance.

Twenty minutes later, he'd had enough. He headed out. His next stop was at the other end of the city, at the morgue.

He strolled in, displayed his badge, and asked for the ME. The desk officer pointed boringly.

"I was waiting for someone, but not you," the ME sniped.

"And here I was, thinking you still exist amongst the living," Rory shot back, parking on a seat opposite the morbid anatomist in his small, congested office.

Rory looked around the office to piss off the ME. "What a dump," he voiced.

“Ain’t you dead yet... I mean, retired?” the ME fired back.

“Soon enough, Your Highness,” the Detective chuckled and continued.

“So, what’s this about the guy your team at ID Unit identified?”

“That’s their business, Rory. Mine is to bring them to ‘life’ and you to do...” he demonstrated, waving his hands in the air, “...whatever it is that you do.”

“Who was he?” Rory ignored the jibe.

“Trevor, something or the other. ID Unit and SRT will help you out on that.”

“Who’s in charge there?”

“I’m not my brother’s keeper, sleuth. Do your job for once.”

“Why all this venom, doc?” Rory asked.

The ME’s anger boiled over. “Your last report wasn’t very flattering.”

Rory frowned, trying to recall. “Oh, the young Asian girl who asphyxiated?” Rory stated.

“Yeah, that one.”

“She turned out not to be Asian but suffered from some ailment that puffed out her face, making her seem Asian. That foopah threw everything off,” Rory accused.

“People make mistakes, you know?”

Rory was having none of it. “Of course. But you didn’t have to break the news to the wrong family. I did,” Rory reminded the cantankerous ME, who stood up, signaling an end to the meeting.

“So, who do I see at SRT and the ID Unit?” Rory asked again.

The ME mumbled something unintelligible as Rory left.

“Asshole,” the ME concluded as Rory slammed shut the door.

At his desk at the precinct, Rory had been searching for missing persons for the last ten years without success. He left the office again.

Now walking the streets in the 5th Ward, he visited dives, bars, and shops, asking for and showing a picture of Trevor Russo obtained from the ID Unit. He had no luck.

He decided to call upon an old informant living at a shelter house. “So, Lamar, do you know who this is?”

The snitch took a long look at the black-and-white picture. "A Ben Franklin would be nice right about now, Dick."

"Are you hustling me?" the Detective asked, eyebrows raised.

"Who? Me?"

"Yes, you. Old-timer."

"No. I'm just saying."

"Well?" Rory growled.

"No. I ain't seen Trevor around here. Try the bar around the block."

Rory left and threw the snitch an Andrew Jackson $20 bill.

Two days later, words filtered back to Rory from the snitch with a name: Bernard Russo, Trevor's father, at a downtown hospital with terminal lung cancer. Detective Rory Franco headed out.

Bernard Russo was an old bank robber himself who was forced to retire and shooed in his strong-headed, recalcitrant son for the Houston bank robbery with Kyle Pearse.

Bernard wheeled his IV tree as he walked ahead of Rory back to his hospital room.

"What the hell do you want?" The old robber lobbed an offensive.

Rory calmly sat down, allowing the old codger to settle back on his hospital bed, knowing insensitive conversations often contributed to emotional distress.

The experienced detective used Trevor's name to convey his condolences, showing Trevor's picture.

"Is this your son?"

"What's it to you?"

Rory sobered up, head hung low.

"We found him," the Detective announced. Bernard sneered.

"Where?" Bernard already knew about Trevor's demise when he didn't return home after several months.

"Is he your son?" the Detective asked. Bernard shifted with discomfort on the bed.

"He was quite precocious but meant nothing by it," Bernard offered as he went on a long cough spell.

Rory allowed him to expel his congestion.

"Water?" Rory suggested.

"Yeah."

Rory handed him a glass from the bedside. "Do you know what happened to Trevor?"

Bernard clammed up and faced away from Rory as a stern nurse came into the room and ended the meeting. Rory left

With Rory at the door, Bernard spoke, "Brass Nacchio, Georgia Cartel, may have something to do with my boy dying. But keep my name out of it if you follow through with those bastards."

Rory turned around. "Thank you," he said as Bernard went on another coughing spell, frantically waving Rory away. The detective gently closed the door behind him.

Rory stood outside the door for a few seconds until the cough stopped before he walked off.

Detective Rory Franco spent the next three hours composing his case report in his cubicle. He walked over to his boss's office.

Rory dumped the report on his young boss's desk. "All done, now, leave me out of it. It's DEA's now."

The Chief waved Rory to sit, about to leave, as the Chief perused the report.

The Chief looked up minutes later. "That wasn't so painful."

Rory's lips pursed. "Anyone else could have done it."

"True, but it would have taken longer."

Rory smiled. “You’re welcome.”

He closed the door behind him as the Chief returned to reading the report.

The Chief picked up his phone and dialed a colleague at the DEA.

A month later, Houston police formally handed the case over to the DEA, which was already investigating Brass Nacchio for Fentanyl drug smuggling, working with a Mexican Cartel.

DEA handed the investigation to DEA agent O’Grady.

***

With 10,000 global personnel, the United States of America’s Drug Enforcement Administration (DEA) combats criminal drug networks to ensure population safety, avert violence, and reduce overdoses and poisonings.

The DEA accomplished this by regulating the manufacturing and distribution of controlled, scheduled prescription drugs and listed chemicals. The Operation One Pill Can Kill (OPCK) initiative is the latest foray into drug overdose prevention for Fentanyl.

At the same time, the Special Operations Bilateral Investigations Unit (BIU) focused on international drug trafficking organizations operating with global tentacles in Mexico and Central America, with pivotal deleterious roles.

In 2023, the DEA seized 384 million deadly doses of Fentanyl, or 76.5 million pills, and 11,900 pounds of fentanyl powder.

In 2022, the DEA seized 59 million fentanyl-laced fake pills, three hundred ninety-eight million in deadly doses of Fentanyl, and 13,300 pounds of fentanyl powder.

It was under these horrible backdrops that Agent O'Grady landed in Georgia to investigate and bust the Atlanta syndicate headed by kingpin Brass Nacchio and his two underlings, Blackie, his enforcer, and Alonzo Gaza, who managed his gentleman's club, Alladin.

But O'Grady himself had "living" skeletons in his closet.

O'Grady recently returned from an eighteen-month undercover assignment in Peru, only to find his wife gone. They were childless. He refused counseling and argued with his boss that a new assignment would suffice.

O'Grady's boss, his friend, and a DEA lifter counseled him. "You're in no psychological frame of mind to take on a new assignment right now, OG."

O'Grady sulked, scratched a five-day stubble, and looked up dolefully at his boss. "I need this. The alternative is even worse."

His boss sat forward. "Stop that self-pity, OG. It's unbecoming."

O'Grady sat up straighter. "This job is the only thing that's keeping me alive..."

His boss jumped off his chair and walked behind O'Grady, who was sitting down. "Are you threatening something?"

O'Grady turned around. "Not particularly. I'm just not ready to do nothing."

His boss patted him on the shoulder and returned to sit behind his desk.

He leaned forward. "Take two weeks off. If you haven't eaten your gun by then, we'll talk."

O'Grady looked up at him, brooded, and left.

Outside, he lit a Marlboro with a silver lighter as he walked to the parking lot.

O'Grady grew his beard, which angled his oblong face, hiding his adoring chin cleft. At least, that's what the rumor was.

He walked into Alladin and saw Sylvia Pearse. He was smitten.

He gravitated towards the stage where Sylvia was gyrating awkwardly, but none of the suckers watching cared about that. O'Grady wielded dollar bills just like the rest, waiting to tuck them into her dental floss of a panty. O'Grady's eye somehow locked with Sylvia.

"Hi," he lamented as she glided off.

"Shit," he said in embarrassment.

He was back the next night and the next, all days, until he was able to engage Sylvia, starting with deliberately overpaid lap dances.

"I ain't fucking you..." Sylvia complained when he thrust a sheaf of bills at her as she ground on him.

"No worries, I like you, lady. What's your name?"

"I ain't no hooker."

"I didn't say you were..."

She interrupted, "Then, what's all this coming in here every night? Your googly eyes are always on me."

"So, you did notice I was looking." O'Grady was pleased.

"It was obvious and pathetic." She ground even harder.

"Yeah... just like that, baby," cooed the lawman.

She stood up and walked off.

"Shit." O'Grady followed but stopped when Sylvia started talking to Alonzo.

O'Grady left the club. He lit a Marlboro with his silver lighter as he walked off.

Three weeks later, after the daily grind at Alladin, O'Grady won Sylvia over for dinner.

"You look lovely," O'Grady expressed as Sylvia parked opposite him at a snazzy downtown Atlanta eatery.

"So, what do you want from me?" She lay into him as soon as she arranged herself, sitting and wearing a flattering red chiffon dress that accentuated all her girly curves.

"I love your dress and..."

"Yeah, yeah, yeah," she cut him off.

"Who's the guy you're talking to the other night?" he asked. He already knew it was Alonzo Gaza.

"My boss. What do you want?" she asked again, looking and arranging the cutlery absent-mindedly.

"Is he anything else, like a boyfriend?"

She looked up. "What's that to you?"

"I wouldn't want to trespass."

She laughed. Her laughter was heady to O'Grady.

He smiled charmingly. "I like you," he said.

The meals arrived. Sylvia dug in with gusto as he played with his steak.

“I’m new in town and don’t know anyone or anywhere. Can you show me around?”

She looked up with a mouthful. She almost seemed as if she was attempting to be as unattractive as possible, which made her more endearing to O’Grady.

“Slow your roll there, mister. I don’t know you,” she quipped, shoveling more food into her mouth.

“I plan to correct that,” he said.

She stopped eating, looked up, and smiled brightly for the first time.

The following week, they took on a movie and had dinner again.

Chapter 14

A month later, she was in his motel room.

Before she arrived, he had prepared a video of the Houston bank robbery, obtained from the Houston police, showing Trevor Russo's face and the getaway skirmish before the video abruptly ended when the getaway car was out of frame.

Sylvia's happy ambiance vanished as she picked up her purse and headed for the door.

"You know that was a robbery scene you just saw. Right?"

She stopped at the door and turned around. "You are a party pooper."

O'Grady's voice became stern. "Kyle Pearse, your brother, drove the getaway car, and the face you saw on the screen was that of a young man, Trevor Russo. His body and two other remains were dug up at an abandoned warehouse."

Sylvia's shoulders slumped as she returned to the room. She collapsed on a sofa as far away from O'Grady as possible.

"So, now I know what you are all about," she spat.

O'Grady, now all granite, stood over her. "You can prevent your brother from going to the electric chair by working for me."

She frowned. "Doing what?"

"I need information on what your boss and crew are doing."

She arose with vehemence. "Like a snitch?"

He shrugged. "That's one way to look at it, but a better way is to think of it as saving a life, Kyle's."

She picked up her purse and busted out of the motel room.

Sylvia and Alonzo's relationship had once again returned to the pre-slug/stab condition, where they seemed to tolerate each other, especially when smoking dope and doing lines.

Thus, Sylvia now had a problem figuring out where to put the microdot spyware O'Grady had given her...

"What am I supposed to do with these?" she asked O'Grady at a follow-up meeting a week after he confronted her with footage of Kyle's bank robbery getaway.

“Simply open the back of Alonzo’s phone, put it anywhere there, and close it back up,” he said.

“That simple?” she wondered out loud.

“Yes.”

They were in an alleyway behind a McDonald’s five miles outside Atlanta. She abruptly turned around and stomped off.

A few feet away, she dumped the bouquet O’Grady had brought for the meeting into a trash can, knowing he was watching.

The DEA agent wasn’t pleased... He puffed his anger away on a Marlboro.

At midnight in their apartment, Sylvia got out of bed beside Alonzo. She paused to ensure he was asleep and reached for one of Alonzo's three phones.

She was momentarily confused as to which one to pick. She picked one and headed to the bathroom.

Two weeks later, she met O’Grady outside Atlanta again as he’d demanded.

He wasn’t standing against a wall in the back alley like before. Instead, he pulled up next to Sylvia, walking down the path, scaring her.

"Watch it, asshole," she said before realizing it was O'Grady driving.

He motioned her to get in the car, a ribboned box of an expensive To'ak, Ecuadorian chocolate, on the passenger seat. She eyed it, eyed him, lifted the box, and sat—the chocolate box on her lap.

"Where are we going?"

"You'll see," he said as he headed for the highway.

"I gotta return in three hours and have a show."

"No worries." He stole a cagy look at her and stepped on the gas, hard.

She stared at him curiously. "You're doing a hundred. What's the rush?"

"You wanted to be back on time." He tried to be jovial, but she was not buying it.

They arrived at Amicalola Falls, and the waterfall wowed her.

"That's amazing," she said, staring at one of the seven wonders of Georgia.

"I knew you'd like it," he said as he walked her to the food truck thirty minutes after their sightseeing. He had refrained from talking shop until then.

As they waited for their taco orders, he asked, "Did you plant the bug as I showed you?"

“Yes, but only on the one phone; he has three of them.”

“Shit,” O’Grady swore loudly, attracting onlookers.

“I’ll get you two more.”

“I don’t think so,” she said, walking away as their meals arrived. O’Grady threw dollar bills at the truck without taking the food and chased after Sylvia.

At the car, he laid into her. “This is not some game, Sylvia. Lives are at stake with what your people are doing…”

She spun around to face him. “They’re NOT my people. I dance and bare my tits and ass to survive, so, please, spare…”

He interrupted a challenge, “Oh, no, no. Don’t do that. You sleep with a gangster working for a Cartel boss, busy smuggling drugs that keep killing people, and you wouldn’t even walk away.”

She began to sob, walked around to the passenger side, and couldn’t open the locked door. She fell to her knees and sat on the grass, crying.

He came around and sat next to her. Silence enveloped them both.

Speeding like a demon back to Atlanta, O'Grady let Sylvia wallow in her self-pity until they were minutes away from behind the McDonald's alley where she'd parked her car.

"Where's Kyle?" he asked. She didn't answer.

He parked behind her car and asked again. "Where is Kyle? I'll issue a BOLO for him."

"A what?" she asked.

"Cops will pick him up."

"I don't know. Since I returned to Alonzo, I haven't seen Kyle."

"Do you talk to him?"

"Not lately."

"If I don't see him by next week, or you cannot tell me where he is, he's toast," he threatened.

Sylvia hissed and left the car, slamming the door hard and leaving the chocolate box behind.

It'd been several weeks since O'Grady's arrival in Atlanta, and he'd not sighted Kyle Pearse despite many photographs he'd taken of Brass Nacchio and his entourage.

He knew where Alonzo was, always at Aladdin, but Kyle and Blackie were missing. O'Grady was getting antsy as he played with his silver lighter before he lit up.

Kyle Pearse sulked silently in the lavish Mexican lounge of Aguapa Mentaje, wondering why he had to go to Beijing.

"Beijing fucking China," he mumbled, and then, staring at the floor, Kyle addressed an angry Aguapa.

"Sir, why would my presence in China affect your operation in any way?"

Aguapa ignored Kyle and stared at Blackie sitting next to him along the long dining table. "Did that pale face say something?"

"Sí, jefe. He…"

Aguapa interrupted, "Es retórica…"

"Lo siento, jefe," Blackie pleaded.

Aguapa turned to Kyle. "Your life belongs to me, so said Brass Nacchio. If I send you to hell, your next question should be, how soon?"

Kyle's head dropped. "I understand. But I can never make Fentanyl for you. I lack such skill."

Aguapa laughed. "You don't have any skill, pendejo." Blackie joined in the ridicule.

Aguapa threw a brand-new Mexican Passport at Kyle's feet.

"Say hello to Yang-Tze in Beijing. Be very careful with him; they eat human flesh in his village."

Kyle picked up the passport from the floor and flipped it open.

He looked up. "Jose Conseco. Really?"

Aguapa and Blackie busted out in extended laughter as Aguapa waved a bodyguard to take Kyle, aka Jose Conseco, away.

It was early in the morning, a week later, when Blackie busted into Kyle's room. "Let's go, Jose," he said, laughing.

Kyle knew it was pointless to protest. He followed with a backpack.

In the car, Blackie lit a joint and passed it to Kyle, still struggling to stay awake. "Toke on this. It'd take the edge off."

Kyle took a deep toke and almost choked to death, tearing up. "Motherfucker," he said when the cough subsided.

Blackie, driving, almost choked himself from laughing. "This is Oaxaca weed, not that shit you smoke back home. They call this baby Napalm."

"You should have warned me," Kyle complained.

"Let me do all the talking at the airport. Remember, this is NOT the USA."

Kyle saw Dollar Bill change hands several times as they passed through the different boarding stages at the airport. Even more surprising was Blackie's access through immigration and up to the aircraft entrance.

Blackie pulled Kyle aside at the aircraft door, out of earshot of other passengers boarding.

"I like you, Kyle. When you meet Yang-Tze, you should keep your eyes open and pay attention to his operations and processes."

Kyle frowned. "Am I some kind of spy for Aguapa?"

"Keep your mouth shut, eyes open, and be humble. They must see you as stupid. That's what Aguapa communicated and why they're allowing your visit."

"But I don't know anything," Kyle protested.

"Exactly," Blackie uttered, walking away, leaving Kyle confused.

As the aircraft taxied, Kyle dreaded the eighteen hours of nothing-bugger coming.

He thought of something and snuck out his phone, which they'd already been told to put away.

He got the voicemail. "Billy, this may be the last call you hear from me... I'm air-bound for China for... I can't tell you that. But, promise me you'll take care of Sylvia and..."

"Please, put the phone away," an authoritative hostess commanded, standing over Kyle until he shut the phone off and pocketed it.

***

Yang-Tze, surrounded by ten men, all similar in age, with a punk-rock hairstyle and covered with tattoos, waved frantically at Kyle Pearse as he broke through the immigration corridor at the Beijing airport.

Yang-Tze spoke in perfect English with a clear American accent. "I thought you'd be Mexican," he said.

Kyle was puzzled. "Why would you think that when you recognized me straight away?"

Kyle instantly knew he just fucked up, being a smart ass. He then laughed it off in a doofus manner. "I'm Jose Conseco, a white Mexican. Ha, got you."

All of Yang-Tze's gang waited to see what their leader would do.

Yang-Tze busted out in laughter, and so did his crew.

They corralled Kyle out of the airport into a Mercedes SUV.

Yang-Tze drove like a madman, reminding Kyle of Blackie.

Three hours later, they arrived at a coal-darkened city, a village named Guye.

Guye was a heavy mining town with fewer than half a million inhabitants that mined coal, quartz, clay, dolomite, and other minerals.

Yang-Tze drove through a dilapidated gate into a red brick compound to let everyone off. They all disappeared except for Yang-Tze. "I'll show you around later," he said, leading Kyle into a building.

At the stroke of midnight, Yang-Tze led Kyle behind a deceptive, poorly constructed facade of a door into a modern manufacturing facility.

"Impressive, right?"

Kyle laughed sheepishly. "Uh-huh, good."

Yang-Tze looked at him curiously. "Surely, you're not as dumb as you're trying to portray. Are you?"

"What?" Kyle bluffed.

Yang-Tze shook it off and continued on the tour.

The vessels were all clean stainless steel with mounted rotor motors. Large weigh scales dotted the place, and enormous exhaust fan pipes were routed back into the building and submerged under a liquid-filled vat.

"We keep our operations tight from the locals," Yang-Tze offered when Kyle's eyes traced the exhaust system.

"Questions?" he asked Kyle.

"I need to sleep, and I'm hungry," Kyle complained.

Yang-Tze laughed. "I got you covered."

They walked off the floor while Kyle mentally filed away chemical posters with formulas posted on walls adjacent to the mixing vessels.

The following day, both men with CSI-like garb and face masks walked into a humming factory. Yang-Tze beamed. "Crazy, right?"

"Right," Kyle agreed with a silly laugh.

Yang-Tze studied Kyle as he took a slow panoramic view of the operation and returned to face Yang-Tze with a devilish smile.

"Come with me; I'll show you something you rarely see."

They walked outside the factory, behind an older brick building, into a smaller room with a steel door. Yang-Tze knocked softly and spoke in Mandarin.

The door opened cautiously to reveal a man, a young man strapped to a chair, beaten to a pulp.

Yang-Tze stepped up to the whimpering man and shot him in the head, dead.

"Let's go," he commanded a stunned Kyle, who was rooted to the spot and unable to move.

Yang-Tze dragged him out. "He was a spy for a rival gang."

Two days later, Jose Conseco, aka Kyle Pearse, was again at the Beijing airport on his way back to Mexico.

Kyle immediately called Billy as he boarded the flight. He got a voicemail.

"I didn't expect you to pick up, but I wanted to let you know I survived Beijing, so no worries about Sylvia. It would be best if you worried about us, though. Come on, man, call me, please!"

Chapter 15

Aguapa Mentaje usually avoided the Fentanyl manufacturing floor, but he made an exception when Kyle Pearse returned from Beijing.

The non-assuming, mousy Aguapa's chemist approached the board in a side office at the factory.

"Three precursors to manufacture Fentanyl and its analogs involve the use of specific chemicals:

Norfentanyl, N-Phenyl-4-piperidinamine (4-AP),

and

Tert-Butyl 4-phenylamino piperidine-1-carboxylate (1-boc-4-AP)."

He paused and looked around for questions.

Kyle looked blank, like someone in the wrong place. The chemist continued.

"Please keep in mind that six years ago, two main precursors, N-Phenethyl-4-piperidone (NPP)

and

4-anilino-N-phenethylpiperidine (ANPP),

were placed under international control.

Since then, I've adapted to those alternative precursor chemicals listed above."

Aguapa looked around, focusing on Kyle, to Kyle's discomfort. "Anything to add?"

Kyle shrugged. "No."

Aguapa glared hard at Blackie, who shriveled.

The chemist continued, "We've adopted two general methods here: the Janssen we used in the past, and now, the Siegfried method, which saved us twenty percent on costs when we switched.

There's a third, new method floating around, which is why we've been searching." He looked at Aguapa. "Any luck, sir?"

Aguapa once again turned to Kyle. "Did you see anything while with Yang-Tze relevant to what our expert just explained?"

Kyle shifted with discomfort as everyone looked at him. His shoulder slumped as he disappointed everyone with a "no."

Aguapa turned back to the Chemist. "What kind of savings would the latest new method fetch?"

The chemist inhaled before he began. "The Janssen method had five steps, the Siegfried method had four steps, and it'd been rumored that the latest methodology only had three steps. Each step reduction is at least $1 million in monthly cost savings."

Aguapa abruptly left the meeting, yelling as he went. "Blackie, bring that idiot to my office."

Blackie dragged Kyle, hurrying after their Cartel boss.

At the office, Aguapa stared hard at Kyle. "Do I need to pump you full of truth serum to make you remember something useful from your China trip?"

Petrified, Kyle looked at Blackie for help. Blackie looked away.

"No, sir. I'm not scientific or technical and..." Aguapa interrupted and looked at Blackie.

"Take this piece of shit away. By tomorrow morning, I want answers, and if I don't get what I want..." Aguapa let the threat linger as he waved them out of his office.

An hour into their drinking binge at a local bar, and before they got shitfaced and useless, Blackie felt he had loosened up Kyle enough for him to free-wheel without Aguapa breathing all over him.

"So, you want to tell me you didn't notice anything in China, with that big brain of yours, despite my clue before you left?"

Kyle took a large swig and blurted out, “You know, that crazy Chinaman executed a young man in front of me?” Kyle sadly laughed as he reached for the beer mug. Blackie prevented him.

“We know,” Blackie said. Kyle froze. “What?

“The guy was an Aguapa spy inside Yang-Tze’s crew.”

Kyle sobered up instantly. “Were you guys trying to have me killed, too?”

“No. Gather intelligence, which you couldn’t even manage.”

“Fuck you,” Kyle said as he staggered up, heading to the Johns. He stopped mid-step, returned to the table, and sat down.

He leaned into Blackie. “Come to think of it, I kept seeing a name on the wall in their lab in several places.” He tried to recall the name, running it around in his head as Blackie watched.

“Gupta,” Kyle blurted out.

“What?” Blackie was confused.

“Gupta. I saw that name a few times with ANPP and 4-AP next to it.”

“That’s an Indian name,” Blackie responded lamely. Kyle lurched forward and threw up all over Blackie.

"Motherfucker!" Blackie yelled as he jumped back from more crud still spewing.

"I'm sorry, man." Kyle pleaded as he rushed off towards the Johns, again, Blackie right behind him.

Chapter 16

Billy walked into the soup kitchen dining hall to see Father Joe dolefully. His head hung low, and he was pushing around the food on his plastic plate. His approach went unnoticed until he plumped down next to the sad cleric.

"The food not to your taste?" he asked.

Father Joe looked up and smiled sadly.

"Garcia won again," he said, looking at the inviting omelet garnished to the nth level.

Billy pulled the plate and started eating from it. "Uhm, yummy," he announced, chewing loudly to irritate himself.

"You're terrible, Billy, but I get it." Father Joe rescued his plate but didn't eat it.

"Pray, what ails you, sir?"

"Nothing," Father Joe said.

"What's the nothing then?" Billy asked.

In despair and knowing Billy would never let it go, Father Joe pushed the plate back at Billy, who shook his head, signifying he no longer had an interest in the food.

"I got a letter in the mail the other day from New York."

"Oh?" Billy was now at full attention.

“The office of Land Management of the Office of General Services in New York informed me of the sale of my mother’s property,” Father Joe confirmed.

“Didn’t you want to sell?” Billy asked.

“No. The deed was no longer in my family name and was sold by someone I did not know.”

“I thought Isabella was handling those?” Billy asked, echoing Father Joe’s sister’s name.

“As far as I knew, she was until the letter came.”

“Is she still at the Abbey of Saint Walburga, Virginia Dale, Colorado?” Billy asked.

Father Joe shot him a surprised look. “You still remember that?”

Billy shrugged and sat straighter. “Have you spoken to Isabella?”

“I did, and she said it was God’s will to atone for our criminal father’s ways before he died.”

Billy, alarmed, remembered that Father Joe once confided to him that the rental income from the property was what was sustaining Isabella, even though she lived at a nunnery.

“Is there a recourse?” Billy asked in full earnest.

Father Joe shrugged. “I’m seventy-five years old and don’t have the energy to fight.”

Billy sat back in thought for what appeared to be minutes but were only seconds.

"I will prepare for a New York trip in a week after I close out my latest deals."

Father Joe looked up; his eyes welled up in tears. "Can you help Isabella? Because when I'm gone, that home is all she'll have left."

"I will make it my mission, Father," Billy said in muted anger.

Now adept in the real estate business and fully aware of industry shenanigans, Billy knew what fraudsters were capable of.

Real estate fraudsters swindle senior citizens often, but these scams have taken the depravity to a higher level, using bold tactics to steal equity from elderly homeowners, leaving them extremely vulnerable to foreclosure and financial ruin.

The schemes are wide-ranging, including posing as non-profit groups and homeowner advocates offering free help to gain trust and steal from their victims.

Their targets are often senior citizens who own their homes outright, those less likely to report fraud because they don't know who to report it to, are too ashamed to acknowledge having been conned, or simply don't realize that they have been defrauded.

Most real estate scams include hard money and high-interest loans to those in desperate need of cash. These loans come with hidden fees and onerous terms that entrap borrowers in a cycle of debt.

Equity skimming targets those struggling to make mortgage payments by offering to take over the mortgage payments in exchange for the deed to the property. Once they have the deed and ownership of the home, they evict the victim and sell it.

Title fraud involves fraudsters blatantly forging documents and using false identities to transfer property ownership to themselves. Once they have control of the property, they may sell it or take out loans against it.

Reverse mortgage cons convince seniors to take money out of a home's equity via a reverse mortgage and then allow the con artist to purchase an annuity or annuities for the homeowner.

Realtors defraud elderly homeowners in several ways, but this can be avoided in multiple ways:

- Never pay with cash or wire cash to anyone concerning real estate transactions.

- Personal information like social security numbers should be protected to avoid identity theft.

- Provide personal and financial information only when deemed necessary.

- Never pay anyone advance fees for a Home Loan or Foreclosure Relief, or sign an agreement for a Home Loan that cannot be afforded.

- Never sign a Real Estate or Home Loan Agreement that is clouded in legal jargon, not thoroughly read, or contains blank spaces.

- Never transfer or sign properties to anyone who claims such transfers will help repair credit.

- Never sign a "Power of Attorney" giving rights to owned property or money to anyone not personally trusted.

- Periodically check the property title and immediately act if fraud is detected.

Billy was unsure what flavor of fraud was at play, but he vowed to investigate and resolve it.

***

Autism had been described as madness, ingenuity, mongolism, and other degradative terms that forced Billy to believe all the so-called experts were simply grasping at straws to illustrate the abject lack of knowledge of the infirmity.

Or is it an endowed celestial blessing that avoided the "normal" technical human limitations of living an unencumbered life? Billy subscribes to the latter, which was obvious when he first saw the gorgeous Isabella Fantone.

Garbed in a nun's black outfit with a white headgear hat, similar to those worn in the late 60s TV series "The Flying Nun," starring Sally Field, Isabella appeared majestic as she welcomed Billy to the isolated holy edifice. The facility looked like a nunnery.

Inside, she walked Billy to a stonewalled room with bare necessities: a chair, table, and bed.

“Sit down,” she said curtly with a fickle smile. Billy obeyed despite himself.

“Father Joe says hello,” lamely escaped his lips as she sat on the bed.

“Who?” she asked.

“Your brother.”

“Oh, Josiah,” she confirmed.

The name threw Billy for a second. He’d always thought it was Joseph.

“Drink?”

“No, thank you,” he said, following up with, “Is this your room?”

She seemed stunned by the question. “No, this is a guest room. You’re staying the night,” she declared.

It never occurred to Billy to stay in an all-female nunnery. He’d driven the thirty miles from town but had planned on concluding his business and leaving.

"If it's no trouble," he found myself saying.

"So, what brings you?" she asked without any inflection from the voice, leaving him to believe she was oblivious to the letter sent to Father Joe.

"Your home in New York is up for sale."

There was no response, so he continued, "Did you put it up for sale?"

"Why would I do that? It's Satan's den," she volunteered.

That threw him for a loop, but he played along. "All homes are satanic at one point or another."

His levity fell flat.

"Satan is too sophisticated for the living. They thrive on earthly belongings," she stated flatly.

"Do you still own your family home up in New York?"

Isabella was puzzled. "I want nothing earthly. I have all that I need here."

Billy was stumped momentarily. "But you know you and Father Joe owned the home you both grew up in."

"Yes. But Josiah does what he needs to do with that. He leaves me out of it as I desired."

Billy's frustration remained under wraps as he explored a different tactic since Father Joe had alluded to the fact that Isabella was handling all that had to do with the property.

"The home, I am told, is worth a lot," Billy stated.

"I have all I need here," she insisted.

Billy sat back and smiled encouragingly. "Did you recently sign anything with anyone about the home?"

"I just came out of a month-long vow of silence," she explained.

Billy showed a slight agitation. "Is that a no?"

"Yes."

"Meaning you haven't signed anything?" he clarified.

"No," she said.

Billy's eyebrows furrowed. "I'm sorry, Sister. Is that a yes? You've signed nothing recently?"

Isabella stared at Billy like a petulant child.

"Yes, I did sign something the Mother Superior gave me months ago, but it wasn't recent."

Billy sat back, better relaxed. "Did you read the document you signed?"

Isabella looked at him as if he'd lost his mind. "Of course not. Mother Superior gave it to me."

"Did you keep a copy?" Billy asked.

Isabella's look was aghast. "Why would I do that? Mother gave it to me."

"Can I talk to Mother?" he asked.

"No."

Billy, in confusion, moved his chair closer to her on the bed. She jumped up. Billy waved a surrendering hand and pulled back his chair.

She sat down again to maintain the distance between them.

"Why not?" he asked.

"Mother Superior just began a month-long vow of silence," she concluded and got up.

"I need to go to the chapel. Someone will bring you food. I will not see you again before you leave in the morning."

Isabella walked to the door, leaving Billy in a daze. She turned around at the door.

"Reverend John Kwouk of the Greater Korean church in New York brought the document months ago, Mother Superior said."

"Do you have an address?" Billy asked. But the door had silently closed behind Isabella.

Billy stared at the wall, befuddled.

"Good gracious," he said as his phone rang.

It was Kyle. He routed it to voicemail, letting him know about Kyle's return from China.

Chapter 17

Billy Pearse landed at New York LaGuardia airport early Sunday morning and drove directly to Poughkeepsie to attend the Methodist church founded by Reverend John Kwouk.

Poughkeepsie means “the reed-covered lodge by the little water place,” which feeds into the Hudson River.

Billy went inside, where a congregation of more than 1,000 worshiped. The racial mix was evenly distributed with a slight edge to Asians, presumably Koreans.

He left after fifteen minutes and headed to Father Joe’s home in the Mount Carmel Historic District, where a “Better Build Homes” for-sale sign was on the lawn of the single-family home. He took down the phone number and address and returned to register at a motel to catch up on sleep.

Three hours into his sleep, Father Joe Fantone called. Billy reluctantly picked up.

“Are you jet-lagged from the time change?”

“No, Father, too tired to feel anything. How’s the kitchen?”

“Young Garcia is doing his thing. But I wanted to check in to see if I have any information that can help.”

"Father, can I call you back in about an hour? I need some coffee. Is that okay?"

"Of course, Billy."

Billy slugged around the motel room and waited for room service, which came surprisingly fast. The coffee was also good. He had toast and scrambled eggs. He now felt human enough to think, so he called Father Joe.

"Was breakfast good?" Father Joe asked.

"Yes. But I will hold off on any information until I visit the county office to see what was filed against your property, and then visit the real estate office afterward. For now, I have no clue what the Reverend has to do with anything."

"A Korean Reverend? Surprising. I, however, do know a soup kitchen I helped set up when my mother took sick, and I lived with her for months before she passed," the cleric offered.

"Are you saying the Korean church wasn't there then?" Billy asked.

"No, it wasn't," Father Joe confirmed.

"How long ago was this?"

"Oh, years ago, Billy."

"That's interesting. Anyway, did you speak with Isabella after my visit?" Billy asked.

“It was disastrous, and she accused you of being Satan’s handyman, sending in a sinner, me, to disturb her life. She was pleasant but a little edgy when we spoke,” Billy explained.

“Her mind works differently, Billy. She meant well; it has a way of coming out wrong whenever I’m on the other end with her.”

“Do you know the Mother Superior?” Billy asked.

“No. But I heard good things about Mother Superior, yet she seemed involved somehow.”

“Father, things aren’t always as they seem in real estate dealings. There are too many charlatans, and document interpretation is difficult at best and dangerous at worst.”

“Well, Billy, I’ll let you catch up on your sleep. Call me as soon as you know something.”

“Will do.” Billy hung up.

‘Better Build Homes’ turned out to be a hole-in-the-wall office.

“Can I show you our portfolio?” An enterprising young lass smiled at Billy.

“Is the manager in?”

“You’re looking at her,” she said, surprising Billy.

"Great. The property on Silwa Road in..."

She interrupted, "Already sold, but I have others that may interest you."

"As I was about to say. The 'for sale' sign is still up there, and I'd like to know who bought it."

"Oh. I thought he took the sign down. And as I said, already sold."

"You mentioned a 'he'?"

"Oh, my boyfriend, Larry. He owns the business."

"Larry?" Billy pressed.

"Larry Landon," she completed.

"Can I talk to him, please?"

"Not possible. Larry's fishing in Niagara Falls."

"When is he back?"

She shrugged. "Are you looking to buy?"

"Not exactly. I'll come back when Larry is here. Thank you."

"Okay." She smiled as Billy left.

At the County office, Billy was shown the microfiche, holding details of title deeds for the county, after several minutes of jawboning with a clerical staff member who wasn't sure he had a right to see it, being from California, after scanning Billy's driver's license.

"You don't have these databases on your network?" Billy asked.

The bespectacled clerk looked sideways at Billy, reminiscent of the young girl in a TV ad who said, "Fer-men-ta-tion?" Instead, the clerk said, "Net-work-whaaat?"

Billy gave up and approached the microfiche table. "Jesus," he mumbled as he sat. His phone rang. It was Sylvia, his sister. It went into voicemail.

Three hours later, Billy left with the information he wished wasn't so.

Driving back to the motel, he heard Sylvia's voicemail announcing she was in trouble with some government guy who wanted her to do something she didn't want to.

The cryptic message bothered Billy so much that he tried dialing her twice, but eventually went on to type as he parked at the lodging.

Slugging coffee, Billy Pearse called Father Joe.

"Bad news, father."

"Oh?"

"I found the name of the person who owned the title, but the deed piece was still shady. I will need to go back for further research."

“Isn’t title the same as deed?” Father Joe asked.

“No. The title is conceptual, just a term used to designate who owned the property. Deed, however, is the document that proves physical ownership,” Billy explained further, confusing Father Joe.

“How can that be? Isn’t there a process you go through to get your name on the deed?”

“Yes. Before any property transfer to someone else, the recipient must be identified, the terms and conditions discussed, a change of ownership form completed, and the title on the deed changed.

“It’s always advisable to hire a real estate attorney to prepare the deed, but I always go further to hire an attorney before the process ever begins. Finally, the deed has to be notarized and filed with the county.”

Father Joe sighed loudly. “Was any of these done?”

“It must have. Now, I have to talk to the real estate person to understand who within your family gave the go-ahead.”

“Come on, Billy, no one did.”

“Sylvia could have without knowing,” Billy suggested.

“I doubt that. But I’ll let you do what you do.”

“It gets worse, Father,” Billy said.

“How could that possibly be?”

"They exercised something called a Quitclaim deed."

"I have no clue what you're talking about, Billy."

"Father, I'll try to be as brief and precise as possible. So, please bear with me...

"A quitclaim deed is most commonly used when a property is transferred from one owner to another–such as parents to adult children, or spouse to spouse–without exchanging money.

"What makes it dastardly is that the deed releases an individual's interest in a property without explaining the nature of their interest or rights, and does not contain any warranties or promises of that person's interests or rights in the property, and carries a higher level of risk when purchasing and transferring a property from a stranger, since they do not come with any guarantees or warranties.

"However, that risk evaporates when the transfer occurs between trusted family members. Quitclaim deeds are convenient and efficient when transferring a deed to family."

"I am completely lost and overwhelmed, Billy," Father Joe confessed.

"I didn't mean to bore you with this, but to engender the hill that must be climbed. But I am confident I'll get to the bottom of it."

"Okay, Billy. It's dinner time with the folks. We have a full house today. I have to go."

"Bye, Father."

Billy hung up, a little sad for dragging Father Joe into the minutia, but he wanted to be sure Father understood the risks ahead.

Two days later, at 6:00 a.m., Billy's motel room door opened silently; three men, behind a janitor, entered. Billy jerked up to the intrusion; he couldn't properly see in the dark except for the sliver of light from the door opening.

"What the hell..." Billy reared up and began to protest when one of the three men shoved the janitor out and closed the door behind her. He approached Billy and pushed him back onto the bed as he turned on the bedside lamp.

"Relax, pops, this won't take long," Larry Landon said through clenched teeth.

Billy saw a young, Ivy League-looking, handsome man whose persona differed from the bullying he was currently espousing.

"I heard you wanted to see me, old man."

"Who are you?" Billy asked.

Larry laughed, looking at his two cohorts who had joined in.

"You came to my office about a property on Silwa. What's it to you?"

"My name is Billy Pearse from California, and I am here to resolve a misunderstanding about a property being sold illegally."

The slap came fast, but Billy expected and blocked it. Billy looked meaningly at Larry and bluffed.

"Thus far, the FBI knows I'm here, and the DOJ is not foreign to me either. I also own a fairly successful real estate business in San Diego. You can check me out.

"I understand how 'opportunities' are converted in this business. So, thus far, you can still salvage from going to prison for a long time..."

Larry, taken aback, was about to speak. Billy shushed him and continued,"...but only this one shot.

"I presume you and your girlfriends over there..." Billy pointed to his two accomplices,

"...probably don't know the extent of what this involves. Property theft will easily get you thirty years without parole for quitclaims... Now, get the fuck out of my room."

Billy lifted his cell phone, and Larry's two accomplices fled. Larry was perplexed, unsure of what to do. He, too, finally fled.

Billy, now alone, was shaking after the confrontation.

"Shit, shit..." he kept repeating as he went to the bathroom and puked his guts out.

Billy walked into the church at 4:00 p.m. two days later, assuming the congregation would have dispersed, leaving only the church administrators behind. He was right. An usher led him to the Reverend's office.

"I heard you had a bone to chew," the affable John Kwouk announced from behind an oak desk in a brown décor office resembling a CEO's mahogany office.

The room was bright despite the overwhelming "brownness." The Pastor waved Billy to sit.

"Not a bone, sir, but a rather sordid fat, I am afraid."

The smile disappeared from the Reverend's face.

"Larry Landon?" he evoked.

"Ah, yes. The young, misguided businessman," Billy rattled.

"Youth is such a cudgel in the hands of the uninitiated."

Billy was getting visibly restless for the verbal run around. “Your man, Larry, must refile a form with the county, remove himself from the Silwa home ownership, and…” The Pastor waved Billy to stop. He did.

“Larry’s father is a long-time, supportive congregant for this church and a 3rd circuit judge, so I…” As the Pastor labored on, he waved his hands to represent something befuddling to Billy.

“I hold the judge in high esteem, and when he suggested I help his wayward son with a seemingly simple affair of talking to a fellow clergyman, I obliged.”

Billy, in confusion, understood what the Pastor was attempting to communicate, but needed clarity.

“Are you saying you were blindsided in the cohort to steal a deed?”

“That’s rather a strong accusation, Mister Pearse. Suffice it to say, I, as a pastor, will never collude in any nefarious endeavor.”

“So, you didn’t get the Mother Superior at the nunnery to sign a document that invariably robbed the Fantones of their property?”

The Pastor sighed loudly, walked off behind his desk, and sat beside Billy. “Yes, I did, but it was under a grave pretense, as I’ve now come to learn.”

“How did it all come about, sir?” Billy asked.

A lady walked in with a platter of steaming tea from an English porcelain kettle, a jar of milk, sugar, and two quaint mugs.

The pastor poured for both. “Sugar?” he asked.

“No, black and no sugar, please,” Billy confirmed.

After the ritual of 1st tea sips, the Pastor returned behind his desk and leaned towards Billy.

“Here’s what I know…”

Young Larry Landon, estranged from his father, attempted to make his way after his father disowned him and left him penniless after graduation from Yale. Left dangling, he floated a real estate company with two friends, the two young dotards with whom he accosted Billy at the motel, concentrating on Airbnb, renting to out-of-towners.

They located the Fantone home under rental at the time, and after months of no intervention from Isabella, they saw an opportunity that eventually led to the quitclaim fraud...

Billy wasn’t buying the circumflected argument but pretended otherwise.

“How did you convince the Mother Superior to sign the title over?”

“I didn’t. I offered a ‘donation’ of $5,000 to the nunnery on behalf of a benefactor, and that was that.”

"And you didn't think that was shady at best?" Billy challenged.

"When a respected judge asked to help, I obliged. But now, I see the folly," the pastor confessed.

"Did you talk or confer with Isabella Fantone?" Billy asked.

The pastor drew a blank. "Who?"

Billy, in disbelief, sighed and leaned back. "Now what, Reverend?"

"After Larry's attempt at bold-facing you at the motel, he stopped by my home and begged NOT to involve his father but to resolve this as long as he gets his capital outlay back."

"Not happening, pastor. I will give you and your team a week to divest this sordid affair and return the ownership to the Fantones.

"I expect the deed in the mail to Father Fantone with all encumbrances alleviated. Only then will this be over. I will then rescind my complaints at both the FBI and DOJ."

Billy left abruptly and received another call from Sylvia, which he left on voicemail. It read... "I need help, Billy. Please call me. Please."

Father Joe received the duly notarized deed to his inherited home two weeks later.

Chapter 18

Billy went to a park after Sylvia's last call.

"Why wouldn't I talk to my siblings and yet am junketing around all over the place for others?" he asked himself, watching ducklings behind a mother duck wading in the park lake before him.

Then, he stood up and walked away toward home. He saw a school bus with flashing red lights near the condo, causing a mini traffic jam. Then, an amazing thing happened when the school bus door opened.

A three-year-old girl with a mini backpack exited and looked around, then saw her mother and her four-year-old brother walking towards her.

As soon as the two children saw each other, they began running fast, albeit awkwardly, towards each other.

They hugged with abandon, laughing and carrying on, giddy at seeing each other before their mother arrived.

That was when Billy decided to end his isolation from those he loved, especially his siblings. He now needed the courage to make the first move.

***

Sylvia walked into O'Grady's motel room in Atlanta for their next meeting. But she wasn't thrilled to be in such close quarters with the DEA agent and was surprised to see a table with lit candles, food, champagne chilling in a bucket, and flower décor.

She frowned and plunged onto the sofa far from the splashy table.

Standing by and watching, O'Grady had disappointment written all over his face.

"At least, wow, the effort, Sylvia."

"Who and what's this for?" she scolded.

"Are you kidding? You, of course."

She giggled with derision. "It's like a pimp trying to get one on the house but then expects payments afterward?" O'Grady came to sit next to her. She got up.

"Are you calling me a pimp?"

Sylvia lay into him, standing akimbo. "You're no different. You bring me flowers and chocolate on the one hand and, on the other, threaten to throw both my brother and me in jail. What do you want from me?"

"I want us to be friends and partners fighting crime. Do you know..."

She interrupted, "I don't want any part of that. Why am I here? I have a show in a couple of hours."

Deflated, he blew out the candles and moved the meeting to the other side of the room with a desk.

Now, all business. "Did you put the bug in all his phones now?"

"Yes." She was irritable but more relaxed than earlier.

"Have you located Kyle, or will he go on BOLO before you leave?"

"When am I going to get out of your clutches, O'Grady?"

"Kyle?"

"Mexico," she yelled.

"Doing what?"

"How the hell should I know? He tells me nothing," she confessed.

The rest of the meeting followed a similar pattern: he tried to be nice, but she got angry and sad, cried, and bolted.

The uncomfortable truce between Sylvia and Alonzo had significantly improved after the coma and stabbing, such that they sat in their lounge smoking and snorting coke.

She occasionally leaned on him as they cackled to innocuous flat jokes that seemed funny in their warped, doped minds.

Alonzo commented, talking about O'Grady. "I noticed a creepy guy that popped out of nowhere who had been spending a lot on you."

Sylvia pretended not to care. "He's one of many of my fans. Are you jealous?"

He slowly moved in on her, and she allowed him to kiss her. New romance soon blossomed, and they moved to the bedroom.

The following day, things got testy again as they breakfasted. It was a Monday morning, the only day Alladin was shut down.

"Don't get mad, Sylvia. Since the adoption thing fell apart, brass wants to know what happens next."

Her chewing stopped. "Like what?" she asked with a mouthful.

"Anything to pay back the twenty grand Brass had spent on you so far?"

She flashed him a fierce look. "On us, you mean?" He got up from the kitchen table.

"He doesn't see it that way. You owe him twenty grand because you're not bringing in as much as the other dancers, and the adoption..."

"Yeah, yeah, yeah," she interrupted and followed him to the lounge.

They began smoking again.

"You should get pregnant," he suggested.

"For the third time? You're crazy," she said, pulling a long toke.

"You hate kids, so what difference does it make?" Oh, you mean trafficking the kid?" she asked, stunned.

"Four hundred K, and you're free to blow this joint, Alladin," he uttered in a lower voice.

"But it's a baby!"

"But you hate kids!" he insisted.

She walked off. "I gotta take a shower."

Her phone rang when she returned to the bedroom after the wet down. It was Kyle.

She locked herself in the bathroom again and told Kyle about O'Grady and that the agent knew he was in Mexico, but she didn't tell him he had made her bug Alonzo's phones.

Kyle poopooed her worries, claiming the Cartel bosses, Brass and Aguapa, had all the South Coast DEA agents in his pocket.

"Aguapa, who?" she asked.

"Nobody," he said.

She hung up when Alonzo knocked on the bathroom door.

"I gotta pee, babe," he complained.

***

Aguapa Mentaje watched Valencia, his only child, his daughter, his world, frolic on a large white filly in the vast horse corral from the panoramic window of his isolated property, his criminal lair, in Valle de las Palmas located between two hamlets, Espuela and Seco in the municipalities of Tijuana and Tecate, Baja, California, Mexico.

Shirtless, Kyle Pearse walked along the corral, outside the fence, with two sacks of chemicals on either shoulder he'd just rescued from the pile in the warehouse several yards away from the factory.

Glistening with sweat and exhaustion, he was oblivious to Valencia stealing glances at him as Aguapa watched his daughter ogle the "Negro."

"Pendejo," he said out loud as he left the window in anger.

Aguapa had commanded Blackie to ensure Kyle worked as a material handler for the Fentanyl manufacturing manager, drawing a chuckle from Blackie.

"¿No te gusta el Negro?"

Aguapa had walked away with boisterous and guttural laughter.

Valencia glanced away and kicked the horse into a running gallop just before Kyle looked up instinctively to see her watching him.

It was dark at the hacienda when Valencia approached her father. “Papá, ya no soy una niña.”

She stomped away from him, attempting to dissuade her from venturing farther out of his comfort zone.

“Why can’t your friend come to dinner here?” he suggested.

She scowled at him. “Papa, she was my best college friend and mate before you sent your goons to ward her off. I’m just now trying to bring back our friendship.”

“Bueno, demándame por amarte, cariño,” he shot back.

“I’m going, papa, whether you like it or not, or I will move out.”

“Eres igual a tu madre, obstinada como una mula.”

“¿Qué acabas de decir, papá?”

“You’re just like Juanita. Strong-headed.”

Valencia halted and turned around.

"You never mentioned Mama's name. Why now?"

"I'm worried sick about losing you, too, mi hija."

Valencia walked back to her father. "You adored Mother for her impulsiveness and once told me that's what you loved most about her."

"Eso es cierto. Pero es posible que eso haya hecho que la mataran."

"El amor no mata a papá; el miedo sí", she concluded.

Aguapa put his arms around his daughter, knowing he'd lost the argument.

"Al menos, deja que la gente te acompañe y te proteja," he pleaded.

She stayed in the embrace and looked up at her father with love.

"More people than you already have always been following me around?" she asked.

He pushed her back to see her nice gown. "Si, cariño," he admitted.

She pirouetted off him, grabbed her purse, and walked towards the door of the large hacienda.

"Adiós, papá."

Valencia's entourage included her driver in a sedan with her and two SUVs with two bodyguards each, plus Blackie, whom Aguapa had conscripted to keep his daughter safe.

Blackie forced Kyle along, who didn't complain the moment Valencia's name was mentioned. Blackie had stared at him with sorrow.

"You got the hots for the Latina?" Blackie cajoled. Kyle ignored him as he lodged himself on the passenger side of a black sedan.

"Are you gonna drive or be up my ass all day?" Kyle asked.

Blackie laughed and jerked the car several times just to be annoying.

"Real mature," Kyle observed as they followed Valencia's protective detail from Valle de las Palmas, which soon flowed into the busy Highway 905 traffic heading to downtown Tijuana.

Unbeknownst to the Valencia crew, but always expected, five pursuing vehicles discreetly tailed behind in four SUVs and a sedan.

Such a fleet of vehicles had become a common scene in the Cartel-controlled cities across Mexico, often trapping unsuspecting innocent bystanders in between gang wars.

...Ten years earlier, as Aguapa Mentaje was building up his business amongst the second-tier Cartel groups in Mexico, then living in Sinaloa, he drove to town with his wife and bodyguard to celebrate a new deal won against a fierce competitor. Fearless and cocky, he committed the unforgettable sin of underestimating an angry rival.

The rival and his team cornered him after the fete with a hail of bullets.

Aguapa's wife went down bloody, while Aguapa sustained multiple injuries but protected his young daughter, Valencia, with his body, lying atop her as bullets rained down before his paid Federales showed up to save the day.

The story goes that "El Choco," "The Crash," an underboss at the Los Zetas Cartel, vied with Aguapa Mentaje, also an underboss at the same Cartel, for the first underboss position, a level just below the Cartel's overall honcho.

Then Aguapa played dirty by covertly importing a Bosnian mob to pose as raw-material suppliers to El Choco, and the mob disappeared with millions of dollars, which threw El Choco off the running against Aguapa Mentaje.

Months later, El Choco's men caught up with the Bosnian crew in Sofia and tortured them to death before they could confess who hired them. However, the documents and voicemail indicated Aguapa as their employer. Aguapa denied it but won the under-boss contest. Thus, the bitter, bad blood between the two future Cartel leaders began.

El Choco's business dwindled as the years passed, but he was tough and hung on. The only thing that kept him going was revenge against Aguapa, and his relentless pursuit of vengeance has been ever since. First, he took out Aguapa's wife but failed to kill Aguapa, and then...

As Valencia dined inside the restaurant, the opposing team fanned out. SUV-1 guarded the north side of the alleyway behind the eatery, and SUV-2 guarded the south side. Both were far out enough to arouse any immediate suspicion. SUV-3 and SUV-4 took a similar stance in front of the restaurant, far enough off.

Their first sedan loitered across the road from the restaurant, waiting for Valencia to exit.

Aguapa's SUV-A stood guard in front of the restaurant, with one bodyguard outside the vehicle alert and the other behind the wheel, engine running—the same protocol observed by SUV-B prominently in the alleyway behind the restaurant.

Valencia's driver was in front of the restaurant door, engine running.

Blackie, smoking, parked two hundred yards behind Valencia's car.

Chapter 19

All hell broke loose when Valencia stepped out with her friend.

After they hugged, the friend got into a cab and drove off. Valencia opened the back door nearest the restaurant to enter when bullets started flying from SUV-4 as it sped up.

Aguapa's bodyguards from SUV-A responded while the driver waited for Valencia to get inside fully, but it was too late; SUV-4 sped up and rammed Valencia's driver. A loud, indiscriminate bullet became the order of the day.

Blackie sped up; Kyle was in a daze, just watching, bamboozled, as Blackie rammed SUV-4 from behind, getting all bloody when his head slammed onto the dashboard. The same fate befell Kyle. They both scrambled out of the vehicle and ducked behind it to avoid being shot.

As the gunfight progressed, SUV-1 and SUV-2, in the alleyway behind, fought fiercely with Aguapa's men in SUV-B, preventing them from going to the front of the restaurant to help.

In front, the attacker's sedan moved in towards Valencia's car. A man with a gun got out, ducked, and weaved towards Valencia's car, opened her door, and dragged Valencia out. Screaming, scratching, and fighting,

Valencia resisted but was no match for the gunman. Blackie and Kyle, pinned down, watched the macabre scene.

Kyle ran off from the safety behind the sedan next to Blackie, towards the gun-wielding assailant dragging Valencia by her hair. A bullet hit Kyle in the leg, but he jumped at Valencia's legs and held on, stopping the dragging.

The assailant tried shooting Kyle in the head to end the menace, but kept missing as Kyle was shifty. He could also have shot Valencia in the head, but El Choco would have killed him, too, because El Choco wanted Valencia as a bargaining chip with Aguapa.

Kyle, now hit with several bullets, wouldn't let go. Emboldened, Blackie sprang towards Kyle, guns blazing. The gunman retreated.

Valencia went nuts, jumped the gunman from behind, knocked him down, and started punching, scratching, crying, and yelling.

The gunman threw her off easily, recovered, and was tempted to shoot her, but instead ran off.

She returned to Kyle, bleeding everywhere.

Then, a chorus of sirens permeated the air.

All the opposing SUVs fled the scene as two federal vehicles arrived, shooting indiscriminately in the air.

Kyle collapsed, bleeding profusely, as Valencia, with scrapes and scratches, tried to keep him from going unconscious by talking to him, holding his head in her lap, and kneeling on the asphalt.

Then the ambulance sirens grew louder as they approached the quiet, eerie scene.

Blackie, wielding his gun, pranced back and forth, waiting for the next attack as Aguapa's SUV, from the alleyway, arrived.

Ten minutes later, an ambulance carted Kyle away, Valencia beside him as EMTs hooked Kyle up to medical equipment and performed first aid to keep him alive.

Kyle Pearse was in a coma for a week and in surgery for sixteen straight hours, with half his body's blood volume lost once he regained consciousness.

Six bullets were removed.

Two were in Kyle's leg, one in his back, one in his arm, and two in his abdomen. The only good news was that nary an organ was damaged beyond repair and healing.

The prognosis at the Traumatología y Ortopedia hospital in Tijuana, the best in Baja, was encouraging, pegging recovery at three months.

Valencia and four bodyguards moved to a safe house in Baja; Valencia was hardly at the house, always beside Kyle at the hospital, in his private room as he recovered.

Aguapa never visited.

Valencia didn't speak to her father again after confronting him about not visiting.

"El Negro no es mi familia, tú sí," he said when she confronted him.

"But he saved my life, Papa."

"He was foolish. The bodyguards would have saved you, too."

"Ya no eres mi padre," she declared, busted out of the hacienda, and moved permanently to Baja.

Three weeks after the shootout, Kyle, still hooked up to beeping hospital equipment, woke up to find Valencia curled up next to him on the bed.

Kyle just kept staring at her until she opened her eyes.

"Hola, mi héroe," she said.

He looked blank, oblivious to what she had just said, except for the "hola" part, but he smiled. She snuggled up further into him. He winced.

She was alarmed momentarily. "Are you in pain?"

"Nada," he said.

She laughed quietly. "Your Spanish sucks."

He smiled and winced again from the pain.

"Should I call the doctor?"

"No, just stay right here," he said.

She smiled and began to sob. "Those pendejos were gonna kidnap me, Kyle."

He smiled at her. "That's the first time I've heard you say my name."

"Kyle, Kyle, Kyle..." she repeated as he allowed her to snuggle up even more.

"I have to breathe, Valencia."

"Later, mi amore." But she relaxed her hold a little.

Kyle walked out of the hospital four weeks to the day and stayed with her at the Baja safe house.

Blackie was a constant visitor and a huge pain in both their asses as love blossomed and flourished.

A month later, Valencia brought a group of official-looking people, including a judge, a court clerk, and a witness to the house, including the friend she had dined with at the shootout.

Valencia and Kyle got married in secret, with all attendees swearing. Blackie was not included in the clandestine nuptial.

The following morning, Valencia went on a violent vomit stretch, scaring the crap out of Kyle until she confirmed she was pregnant.

“No one must know about this, or we may both get…” she made a sign of throats being slit.

“But you will eventually show,” he reminded her.

“I’ll deal with that when the time comes, cariño,” she uttered bravely.

Kyle could not hide his trepidation despite the brave facade he presented.

“We’ll be fine, you’ll see,” she predicted with infectious enthusiasm, which he falsely echoed.

***

For the past three months, O’Grady had followed Brass Nacchio to restaurants and basketball games on three other occasions without making any major headway. First, he went to a restaurant in Upper Atlanta, where he met with two Italians in suits.

But their conversations were so benign that he gained nothing from them. He had many pictures he'd dispatched to his boss, but yielded nothing—just another set of crooks featured on an ever-expanding link-chart work-board.

Then he saw Brass at an Atlanta Hawks game with the LA Clippers, where Brass yucked it up with some of the pros after the game. He freely got autographs and left without meeting anyone under O'Grady's radar. But now he was at the Chattahoochee Hills Bouckaert Farm horse racecourse.

O'Grady watched Brass settle at the front railings, directly watching the milieu before the last race began, fifteen minutes away. O'Grady decided to place a bet for the heck of it.

As he approached the betting hall, O'Grady saw the back of someone he thought he recognized, but thought the odds were impossible. He lightly tapped the man on the back of his shoulder.

It was who he thought it was. "Maverick?"

In a light, dark summer coat, the man wore a thin black tie and two pens stuck in his shirt pocket. He turned to face O'Grady.

"O'Grady?" Maverick McNealy responded with surprise.

They both shook hands heartily.

“You’re the last person in the world I expected to…” O’Grady began to say when Maverick corralled him away from the hall to a secluded corner. O’Grady followed with trepidation.

“What? Are you hiding from someone?”

“No. But let’s take it somewhere less crowded.” Maverick suggested.

Maverick McNealy didn’t justify his name as “Maverick.” If anything, he should’ve been named “Poindexter.”

The bespectacled man looked nothing like the government agent he was. Maverick was an investigator for DHS–Department of Homeland Security–when O’Grady last encountered him in Washington, D.C., for a terrorist symposium sponsored by the White House. He was then the lead for DHS, under the arms of the Office of Intelligence and Analysis, TOI&A, on the trail of terrorists globally.

“What in the hell are you doing here?” O’Grady asked.

“Working.”

O’Grady frowned. “In the field?”

“Yeah. I transferred a year ago when the new DHS Secretary arrived and defuncted TOI&A. I had a choice: field or take my thirty.”

“You took the field. But you stick out like a...” O’Grady trailed off.

“Like a sore thumb,” Maverick completed.

“Yeah,” O’Grady agreed and continued, “Why are you here?”

Maverick countered, “Why are YOU here?”

O’Grady paused ever so slightly, weighing tactics. He decided on a frontal approach.

“Brass Nacchio.”

It was Maverick’s turn to halter. “Atlanta Cartel?”

“Yeah, he’s out at the railings with another character I don’t know.”

Maverick smiled. An ugly smile displayed a set of tobacco-stained teeth. “Aguapa Mentaje.”

“Who?” O’Grady is now at full attention.

“The Tijuana Fentanyl King,” Maverick proudly announced.

O’Grady decided to hold his cards close to his chest. “What do you have on him?

“A recent charter months ago indicated a man used false identification to visit China and meet people under our radar,” Maverick divulged.

“Which man?”

Maverick took out his cell phone and scrolled rapidly to show Kyle Pearse's picture.

"Do you know where he is now? O'Grady asked.

"No. But we know the man he visited in China had a long relationship with Aguapa Mentaje."

"Ah. So that's why you're here?"

"Yeah." Maverick turned and headed towards the railings, O'Grady in tow.

Aguapa Mentaje had taken the trip across the border to let off steam after a blowout with his daughter, Valencia.

"It must be a serious situation to drag you away from Tijuana," Brass Nacchio had said when Aguapa arrived unannounced at a dinner table a week earlier.

Aguapa hadn't crossed the border for a year, deathly afraid of capture.

"Valencia chose the pendejo Negro over me," he lamented.

"Negro? Are you racist now?" Brass had jokingly accused his partner.

"I'm Mexican. How can I be racist?" Aguapa fired back in earnest.

"By calling someone Nigger."

"I didn't. I said Negro."

Confused, Brass smiled. "Same difference."

"Oh no. I hate that Negro because Valencia hasn't been the same since you sent him to me."

"Is it my fault now?" Brass wanted to know.

"Yes," Aguapa confirmed and continued. "He's just disrupted my quiet life."

"Did he do something to upset you?"

"Haven't you been listening? He took Valencia from me," Aguapa repeated.

Brass sipped his drink slowly and deliberately. "Valencia is a grown woman, Aguapa!"

"She's still my daughter. I no longer want to talk about this anymore." Aguapa waved over his bodyguard, who brought two fat cigars to both master crooks.

"Ha... Cubana. Mi favorito," Brass yodeled as he lit up. Aguapa smiled for the first time.

"I know what'd cheer you up," Brass volunteered.

"What?" Aguapa asked as he blew a thick cloud of smoke.

"Chattahoochee Hills Bouckaert Horse Farm."

Once back at the hacienda, Aguapa's irritation returned. Irate, he ordered Kyle forcibly brought to him.

Valencia saw two fierce bodyguards forcibly enter her small Baja compound, pushing back the four bodyguards who worked for her father, whom Valencia had hired. But her four security detail knew well enough not to grapple with the Aguapa men. Thus, they resisted the encroachment in a lackadaisical manner and then relented.

"Señora, su padre quiere que Kyle regrese a la hacienda," announced the lead bodyguard, respectfully, knowing tact would be paramount.

"Por qué?" she challenged as Kyle watched.

"No sé," the bodyguard responded.

Valencia's belly had not begun to show, even though she now had a little belly pouch. Kyle stepped between her and the large bodyguard.

"You should leave now."

The lead bodyguard looked at his accomplice, who approached Kyle menacingly. Valencia cut him off and stood in his way.

The lead bodyguard softened his approach. “Señora, no quiero estar aquí. Pero tu padre no es un hombre fácil de enfadar. Por favor, ayúdame aquí.”

Kyle, oblivious, fidgeted, looking around in confusion. “What? What?”

Valencia placed her hands on him to calm him down. Then, she whispered something in Kyle’s ear. Kyle visibly deflated, slumped his shoulders, and walked away.

“Senora...” The lead bodyguard began to say something when Valencia interrupted him.

“Basta ya. Sólo espera aquí,” she said as she also walked away.

Minutes later, Kyle, all dressed up with a backpack, followed behind Valencia, who defiantly stood nose to nose with the lead bodyguard and spoke with utter intensity. “Sé que estás haciendo tu trabajo—si algo le pasara a Kyle, le pediría a mi padre que te matara. ¿Lo entiendes?”

“Si,” the bodyguard responded and led Kyle away after Kyle kissed Valencia.

The two bodyguards stood on either side of Kyle in front of Aguapa in the hacienda's lounge at Valle De Palmas.

He waved the bodyguards away to give Kyle more personal space.

"Desnúdate, Negro," Aguapa commanded.

"What?" Kyle asked in confusion.

"Take off your clothes," the lead bodyguard interpreted. Kyle stood immobile.

"Are you deaf?" Aguapa asked.

"No. I'm not stripping," Kyle snapped back.

Aguapa bellowed with his guttural laughter as he signaled the bodyguards, who immediately manhandled Kyle, tearing his clothing off him, leaving only his boxer shorts.

Defiant and standing tall, Kyle swore at Aguapa. "You are a shameless bastard. You think I'm afraid of you? Fuck, no, and fuck you while we're at it."

"¿Qué?" Aguapa questioned and rushed into Kyle's face.

Nose to nose, Aguapa spat. "Turn around." Kyle did nothing.

The bodyguards turned him around against his will as Aguapa inspected the bullet wounds, inch by inch, poking at them from the failed Valencia kidnapping.

Aguapa then returned to sit and dismissed the bodyguards.

“Put your clothes back on and sit down.”

Kyle put his tattered clothes back on but refused to sit.

“Sit down,” Aguapa commanded again.

“No.”

Aguapa instructed him, “Tomorrow, you start to train for your journey with the Ilegales.”

Aguapa’s inside assistant smoothly appeared and guided Kyle away as Aguapa’s laughter dominated the large enclosure.

Chapter 20

The constant proximity that had built between Blackie and Kyle initiated the beginning of 'softness' between the two crooks. First, when Blackie tried to get him killed by robbing a gas station in Tucson, Arizona, Kyle wasn't judgmental.

Then, when Kyle selflessly saved Valencia, knowing her father could kill him anytime, he developed a new respect for the Negro, but tried as best as he could to mask the admiration for both their sakes.

Blackie walked with Kyle for what seemed like miles.

Kyle, sucking wind, asked, "Why didn't we drive?"

"Tired, Sunshine?" Blackie ridiculed and then quickened his pace.

"Godamned it," Kyle swore as he drank from the water bottle thrown at him when they left the hacienda an hour earlier, which should have clued Kyle in but didn't.

"Are we there yet?" Kyle asked a few minutes later.

Blackie, in front, stopped. Kyle ran into his back; Blackie turned around.

Both stared at each other and burst out laughing in unison.

"Are we there yet?" Kyle prodded.

Really?" Blackie repeated as he sat down under a lone tree in the desert.

As Kyle sat next to him, Blackie said, "Watch for the copperheads." Kyle shot up as if catapulted. Blackie laughed harder. "Just kidding."

Kyle sat back down, wiped the sweat off his forehead, and inspected the little water in his bottle.

"Are we there yet?" Kyle asked again. Blackie ignored him.

Aguapa Mentaje bought the three-hundred-acre land years after he became the second in command of his Cartel. He had no idea why, but knew property ownership was the way to go.

Twenty years later, the massive multiflora property had a variety of sections utilized for various phases of his business. Today, Blackie and Kyle were deep in the section where illegal immigrants were housed, fed, trained, and prepared for the crossing into the United States.

"I'm beat, man! How much longer?" Kyle asked, laboring behind Blackie.

Blackie pointed over a hill about a mile ahead, where roofs were just beginning to jut out.

"There. Pussy."

"Yeah." Kyle heaved as he lugged behind the seemingly tireless Blackie.

The gun-toting guards smiled as they let Blackie through the front gate, with another at the back, and completed a suspicious run-down of Kyle, who was too tired to care, into the ten thousand square foot walled-off, isolated property.

Inside the compound, a series of five ranch buildings formed a semi-circle, leaving the middle empty. The two visitors were shown into the largest of the buildings.

"Rest up, Kyle. I need to run you through what's happening here."

Blackie didn't wait for an answer. He walked out into an adjacent room.

Kyle looked around the minimalist room, which had a hand-wash sink, a toilet with a door, and a radio on a small table.

Kyle lifted the radio and turned it on as he lay on the bed.

The broadcast was in Russian.

He turned the dial and found a French station.

The next was Chinese.

He turned the radio off and shut his eyes.

Blackie walked in to find Kyle snoring.

He pulled Kyle's legs off the bed, jerking him awake.

"Let's go."

Groggy, Kyle complained, "You just left, man."

"That was an hour ago, dumbass," Blackie corrected.

Kyle followed sheepishly out of the building.

The next building was a jail cell, with guards watching rows of men and women behind bars. There were Indians, Orientals, Africans, and others just sitting dejected in their cells.

"What the hell?" Kyle asked Blackie, who did not react to the room.

"These immigrants made arrangements with Aguapa's partners in their countries that once they're here, a family member will pay for their fare," Blackie explained.

"Why are they imprisoned then?"

"No family member showed up for them," Blackie confirmed.

"So, what's gonna happen to them?" Kyle asked.

"They work it off."

"How?" Kyle was curious.

"You'll see," Blackie confirmed and walked them out.

Outside, Kyle asked. "Why did you show me that?"

"We'll need some of those guys for your trip."

"Trip?" Kyle played dumb. Blackie turned around in anger.

"Why in the fuck do you think you're in Mexico?"

Kyle sulked behind as they entered another building.

The din and stench that greeted them was overwhelming. Kyle covered his nose while Blackie seemed unaffected.

The room was divided into smaller rooms without doors, where women and children lolled around in dejection as multiple children cried and wailed.

The noise should drive normal people crazy, but those inside seemed oblivious to the mental torture.

Kyle tried to walk back out Blackie prevented him. "Don't do that."

"Who are these?" Kyle asked.

"They're the wives and children of those people you just saw in the cells."

"Jesus!" Kyle lamented and continued. "But why do I have to see these?"

Blackie ignored him and walked them back out into the next building.

Here, a man was being tortured by another wearing boxing gloves.

"What did he do?"

"He tried to escape," Blackie confirmed while making professional jabbing and uppercut boxing moves. The torturers found this interesting and copied Blackie's moves.

The torturer approached the victim and landed an uppercut that rendered the victim unconscious.

"Yeah," emanated from Blackie in jubilation. Kyle was allowed to walk out this time.

Outside, Kyle was about to vomit when Blackie stood over him.

"This is Aguapa's world; I am trying to show you."

"Why?"

"Don't fuck up, or you'll end up here," Blackie confirmed and walked away.

***

After O'Grady stumbled upon information from Maverick McNealy about Kyle working with the Mexican

Cartel of Aguapa Mentaje, he knew he needed to go to Mexico.

Still, he found himself reluctant to leave Sylvia behind. He couldn't accept that he'd fallen for the pole dancer but struggled with whether the infatuation was a rebound from his divorce or genuine affection.

With that preoccupation, he walked into Alladin on a Tuesday evening, the first open day of the week for the gentleman's club.

The clientele volume was light just after midnight as he settled near the stage where Sylvia was gyrating.

Alonzo saw O'Grady walk in, tracking his movement straight to gawking at Sylvia dancing.

Alonzo confronted O'Grady. "Are you fucking her?"

"What?"

"Do you want to fuck her?" he rephrased the question. O'Grady turned away.

Alonzo went around to face him. "I've seen you too many times with her. Do you know her?"

"What's it to you?" O'Grady challenged.

"I run this joint. See." Alonzo thumbed his chest.

"Good for you." O'Grady returned to watching Sylvia. Alonzo waved over two beefy bodyguards who soon bookended O'Grady.

"This is how you treat paying customers?" O'Grady complained.

"Something ain't right about you." Alonzo signaled the apes to evacuate O'Grady.

O'Grady raised his hands so they would not touch him and walked out voluntarily.

Sylvia, dancing, saw the whole thing but pretended not to notice. Alonzo thought he caught a glint in her eyes as she saw O'Grady leave.

O'Grady puffed away in anger as he walked towards his car.

Early in the morning, after returning from Alladin, Sylvia took off her clothes at their apartment. Alonzo studied her, and she became self-conscious.

"What?" she asked. Alonzo walked off to the bathroom without answering.

In the bathroom, he stared at himself in the mirror, got angry, and tried to breathe in rhythm to suppress it. He failed.

He walked back to the room as Sylvia took off her panties. He stared again, to her discomfort. She turned away. "What's your fucking problem?"

He moved fast to her and bumped her from the back. She went flying into the wall, headfirst. She yelled in pain, got up, turned around, and lunged at him with her nails out.

"You fucking bastard!" she yelled as she attacked him, which he easily deflected.

She sat heavily on the bed and nursed a large bump forming on her temple.

He saw the swell and tried to approach her. She jerked up, hurried, put on her clothes, grabbed her purse, and blew the joint.

"Where the fuck do you think you're going?" he called after her, but he heard the front door slam.

"Bitch," he said, went to the lounge and grabbed a liquor bottle, sat on the couch, and lit a joint.

He took a large swig, inhaled the dope, and brought out a small pouch of white powder.

"Motherfucker," he said as he laid out lines.

Like O'Grady, Alonzo had grown to love Sylvia but dared not acknowledge the heartache.

His job at Alladin, his inter-entanglement with Brass Nacchio's business, and Sylvia's child trafficking business were impediments to his accepting what was obvious.

Hence, his jealousy of O'Grady threw him back to the same violence that led to the coma and stabbing incidents several months earlier.

Now, shit-faced and high, he threw the empty liquor bottle hard against the adjacent wall. The splinter came at him and nicked his face under the right eye, drawing blood. He felt nothing as he passed out on the couch.

Sylvia ran into O'Grady at the front of his motel, heading out. He turned around immediately when he saw the nasty bump on her head.

"Jesus. Did you report to the police?" he asked.

She walked past him inside and headed to the elevator. He followed.

He was standing in front of the lift. "I'll go with you to the precinct," he volunteered.

She looked at him with a sad, sorrowful gaze. "I need a drink. A stiff one. You got some?"

"He will not stop abusing you unless you put him in jail," he said as they climbed into the elevator.

She used her hand to cover the nasty pink mound growing on her head. "He didn't mean it."

He giggled mirthlessly, which irked her. "You think that's funny?"

“Not at all. But you making excuses for your abuser is funny.”

She scowled at him. “Ain’t you supposed to be making me feel better?”

“By lying to you?” he countered, letting them into the room.

He left and soon returned with a bottle of liquor. It was only 11:00 a.m.

She gulped a full glass of Jack Daniel's.

“Jeez, take it easy.”

She looked at him, thrusting her head bump at his face. “You wanna trade places with the thumping in my head?”

He left and soon returned with ice wrapped in a towel. He tried to place it on Sylvia’s head, but she shifted away and applied the cooling to the swell herself.

She grabbed the bottle and sat heavily on the sofa, drinking directly from it. O’Grady tried to take it from her. She refused.

“Got any weed?” she asked.

He sat next to her. “You forgot what I do?”

“Law enforcement doesn’t smoke dope? It’s legal now,” she announced as if she were proud of herself.

"No, I don't, and you should take it easy on that bottle." The full bottle she started with was already halfway gone. She then reached to kiss him. He didn't resist but wrinkled his nose from the liquor stench.

She put a lot of tongue into the sloppy kiss, surprising the agent, who found himself uncontrollably aroused. She got up and dragged him towards the bedroom.

She woke up on the bed, naked, and held her head from throbbing a headache. She looked at herself naked and looked around the room to see her panties and bra flung all over.

"Oh shit, shit, shit," she said as she crawled off the bed to put on her undies.

She called out for him, "Hey? Hey? Where are you?"

She walked around the small suite, but he was nowhere to be found. Just then, the front door opened, and O'Grady was carrying a brown bag smelling of Chinese takeaway.

"You hungry?" he asked.

She followed him to the table, where he laid out the boxes and cutlery.

"Did we do it?" she asked.

"Do what?"

"You know...?" she asked coyly.

He turned to her. "You gonna eat or what?"

"Did we fuck?" she blabbered.

He stood up, his back ramrod. "That was so crude. Sit down and eat something. It'd help with the headache I know you must be having now."

She held her head on cue and felt the bump that had receded significantly. She looked at him, pointing to the bump. "Did you do something to it?"

He began eating and spoke with mouthfuls, "Old Chinese trick."

"What's that?"

"Tiger balm."

"What?" she asked in confusion.

"Sit down and eat before the food gets cold." She did.

With a few morsels in, she asked again, "Did we fuck?"

He stopped eating and walked off to get water.

"No," he confirmed.

She threw fried rice in his face. "Wasn't I good enough for you?"

"You're plenty pretty, but I'm on duty."

"Your loss," she said.

She went to Alladin that night to dance and made up with Alonzo.

Chapter 21

Sylvia climbed off the stage after one of her most successful sessions with dollar bills stuffed in her body everywhere.

Lately, she'd noticed more ogling from men than usual, but couldn't identify what she did differently so that she could do more of it.

As she descended the steep flight of steps off the stage in a six-inch pump, she felt nauseated and rushed towards the bathroom.

She ran by Alonzo in the tight hallway, who wanted to talk. She waved him off. "Not now."

She barely made it to an open stall and vomited all over the toilet bowl, behind it, and the floor. Another dancer who had just entered the bathroom heard the retching and approached.

"Jesus," the dancer said as she helped Sylvia kneel on the floor and held her long hair up to direct Sylvia's face inside the toilet bowl.

Sylvia vomited some more, waited a minute in her kneeling position, and then signaled to the helper that she was done. The helper lifted her and guided her to a sink to wash up.

"Are you pregnant or something?" the helper asked.

"No, it must be something I ate," Sylvia surmised.

"Okay, I'm on now, I gotta go." The helper left.

A week later, back at their apartment, Alonzo prepped their lounge table to relax on Monday morning, the Alladin shutdown day.

"Hey, babe," he called out to Sylvia.

"Coming, I'm in the bathroom."

"Again?" he complained.

"Must be something I ate," she confirmed as she walked in, sat beside him, and took the lit spliff.

"Hey," he complained, and she snuggled up to him, and he smiled and began to roll another joint. Then, she jerked up and ran to the bathroom again.

"Jesus Christ," he moaned, lighting the new joint.

Meanwhile, Sylvia knelt at the bowl, retching, but nothing came out.

"What the hell? This is getting old," she admonished herself as she cleaned up.

Though she didn't know it yet, Sylvia Pearse was three months knocked up, pregnant.

Sylvia fell apart when she learned from her gynecologist that she was pregnant.

"No, you're wrong, doc."

The doctor laughed. "That's an unusual response. Typically, people will either jump up happily or be mad.

"But I haven't..." Sylvia began to say and then changed her mind. "How long?" she asked instead.

"Three months," the doctor confirmed.

In an awkward silence, Sylvia dressed up as the doctor cleared the examination area and guided Sylvia to the front office.

"Now what?" Sylvia asked.

"The usual, nothing strenuous, better diet, and read up on baby stuff."

Sylvia stared at the doctor as if she'd lost her mind.

"But I can dance. Right?"

"Yes, but not on those terrible high heels, Sylvia. A fall could be devastating."

Sylvia sulked briefly. "Anything for the vomiting shit?"

The doctor wrote her a prescription and set her next appointment.

"Come with your husband next time, Sylvia."

In shock, Sylvia laughed as she collected the papers from the confused doctor.

Alonzo set the kitchen table with white linen, candles, and other decorations to celebrate Sylvia and her pregnancy.

She allowed herself to be pampered as she sat waited upon by her now awkward boyfriend.

"How do you feel?" he asked.

She stared at him funny as she unwrapped the burritos he'd just laid out.

"Like a fat whale about to devour a little minnow."

He stopped fussing and turned around to face her.

"What?"

She laughed.

"I heard that on TV, watching some animal show. What the hell is a minnow?" she said lamely.

Alonzo then settled across from her at the table to unwrap his burritos. "I don't know. Must be some animal."

They ate silently for a while, and she sipped wine with an accusing facial gesture from Alonzo.

"Don't look at me like that. You put the wine on the table," Sylvia snapped.

"Easy, babe. Just be careful."

"Don't mother me, asshole." "Okay, okay." He backed down as they ate in silence

"I should tell Brass that you're pregnant, Sylvia."

She was silent, sulky, and unapproachable.

"Did you hear what I said?" he repeated.

"It's my uterus, not Brass's."

"What?" Alonzo asked in confusion.

"I'm the one pregnant, not him." She gritted her teeth as she stepped away from the table.

"You know what I mean, Sylvia."

"Yeah, yeah, yeah..." she said, heading to the lounge.

"Smoke?" she asked.

"You gotta be kidding," he said.

"Watch me," she replied as she lit a joint.

Alonzo walked in and studied her, astonished. "But the baby, Sylvia?"

"So?" she countered.

"I'm just saying." He shrugged as he sat next to her, rolling a joint.

It’d been months since the encounter between Agent O’Grady and Sylvia Pearse, and she had unilaterally declared his hold on her as verboten.

She’d refused to take his calls, and as he was banned from Alladin, O’Grady sat in his rental car across the street from the club parking lot, watching Sylvia emerge. He slowly cruised to her in the parking lot, scaring her until she recognized him.

Irate, she let loose. “Can’t you take a hint, agent?”

“Get in the car, Sylvia.” She didn’t. Instead, she went around to open her car door.

O’Grady rushed out and forcibly pulled her towards his car's passenger side.

She resisted at first, but then just followed him.

“Be careful, I’m pregnant, you ape.”

He let go of her like a hot potato and stepped back as if she were toxic. She laughed and walked to his car of her own accord while he stood rooted outside.

She stuck her head out of the window. “Well?”

He reluctantly got in and turned to face her.

“Since when?”

“Since when what?” she asked.

He pointed at her belly. “That?”

"What did you want to see me about, agent?"

"Kyle," he lied.

Since their encounter, he'd missed Sylvia and realized his interest in utilizing her as an informant had been a farce the moment he fell for her. Now, he just wanted her to like or care for him.

"You have to leave my brother alone and..." She trailed off when he kept staring at her belly. "Stop that," she said.

"Is it Alonzo's?" he asked.

"You need to leave me alone, agent. I no longer want to help you." She pointed at her belly and continued, "The risk is too much."

Lost for words, O'Grady remained quiet while Sylvia fidgeted all the time. Minutes into the silence, she opened the car door and left.

O'Grady said nothing, only watching her enter her car and drive off.

Frustrated, O'Grady flipped his silver lighter in the air and missed it coming down.

"Yeah," he said as he picked it up from the ground and lit a Marlboro.

***

The United States' southern border with Mexico is over 1,900 miles long, stretching from the Pacific Ocean to the tip of Southern Texas, with 700 of those miles fenced.

As a deterrent, fencing formed part of a larger holistic Homeland Security approach to border security.

Between San Diego and Tijuana, Mexico, there's high double fencing to deter people from crossing illegally. Part of the fence extends along the beach and continues into the Pacific Ocean.

U.S. Border Patrol agents use high-tech surveillance equipment, from motion-sensor cameras to drones to tethered aerostat balloons that fly high over the border, constantly providing a panoramic view.

Tijuana City is located near the Tijuana River, which ends within the river basin and is intermittent over 100 miles on the Pacific coast of northern Baja California in Mexico and Southern California in the United States.

The river drains an arid area along the California/Baja border, flowing mostly through Mexico. For the last five miles, it crosses the border, dumping into the ocean via an estuary.

The San Ysidro entry zone is the busiest Tijuana border crossing and is the most used to get to Baja, California.

It's the first preference among three other San Diego border crossings, including Otay Mesa and the CBX (Tijuana Airport).

Tijuana is known for its rugged terrain, including many canyons, steep hills, and mesas. Large hills in Tijuana include the Cerro Colorado and the Cerro de las Abejas. The hills provide Cartel scouts with a vantage point to monitor activity in the area and track the Mexican military's movement.

On average, crossings from 1,000 to 1,200 daily occur from the ocean to the mountains seventy miles to the east, and it's dangerous to rely on smugglers who often force asylum-seekers to scale the thirty-foot barriers along the border. Migrants have lost their lives falling from the border fences.

Chinese migrants pay anywhere from $20,000 to $35,000 to enter Ecuador and fly to Colombia, or to enter Nicaragua. They eventually arrive in Baja and then cross into Jacume. Others cross into Mexico at Tapachula, travel freely within Mexico, and arrive in Tijuana.

Blackie, like all human smugglers, was armed and linked to criminal groups familiar with the landscape and every route leading to the U.S. border wall.

The Cartel used various devices to deter capture.

They left traps, such as spiked wires on the roads that punctured patrol vehicle tires, and paid off local ranchers who acted as lookouts.

Kyle Pearse and Blackie were back in the hacienda from the desert but were immediately summoned by Aguapa to the house.

Aguapa, on the phone at the window watching horses in the corral, had called Blackie. Blackie arrived with Kyle, and Aguapa dispatched Blackie, leaving just the two of them.

In a surprise move, Aguapa invited Kyle to sit.

Kyle was suspicious but sat at the edge of his seat opposite the expressionless Cartel boss.

“You need to let go of my daughter, Negro.”

Kyle immediately took offense to the term "Negro." He riled up.

“Sit down. I didn’t call you a nigger. Negro means black.”

Kyle searched his face before he sat down again.

“Let Valencia go. You don’t belong in her world,” Aguapa repeated in conciliation.

“You don’t know Valencia, sir. We love each other,” Kyle announced.

Aguapa sat back. “Do you think you’re the first hombre to try and whisk away my only child?”

“We love each other,” Kyle reaffirmed.

“When Valencia turned fifteen after her Quinceañera, a boy not so different from you but Latino stole her heart, only to cheat on her. The pendejo is no longer with us.”

“What?” Kyle asked in alarm.

“I sent him packing,” Aguapa confirmed to allay Kyle’s fears.

“But Valencia and I are…”

Aguapa interrupted, “Valencia knows this business of ours head to toe. She kept the books until you rescued her, and she left. But she will always be part of this business. It’s in her blood.”

Kyle had no response but looked on searchingly at Aguapa, who continued.

“Let her go, Kyle, and I will not ask you again.”

He signaled, and his assistant immediately appeared, leading Kyle out of the house.

Aguapa, on the phone, called Blackie and stood at the window overlooking the horse corral to watch several horses being trained.

Blackie was all smiles as he walked in, but the smile disappeared once he saw Aguapa’s demeanor.

“What do you know about this Negro?”

Blackie fidgeted, unsure where the conversation was heading.

"Not much. Brass asks that I bring him to you to pay off a debt."

"Is he a DEA informant?" Aguapa asked. The question threw Blackie.

"What?"

"Are you sure he's not a plant by the DEA?" Aguapa asked again.

"I don't know, but I don't think so."

"He also enamors you because he saved Valencia," Aguapa stated flatly.

"He almost died, jefe!"

"That could be part of his cover," Aguapa argued.

Blackie shook his head; no, but Aguapa was not buying it.

"The pendejo slinked in here, targeted my daughter, enraptured her, and now I am left with nothing," Aguapa lamented. Blackie remained quiet.

"Say something," Aguapa commanded.

"I think he's clean, boss."

"So, what do I do about Valencia?" the Cartel boss asked. Blackie shrugged.

They remained silent for minutes, and then Aguapa dismissed Blackie, who left in confusion.

"Watch him when you take the trip," Aguapa offered as Blackie walked away.

Chapter 22

Blackie became a little coy around Kyle as they were driven by two of Aguapa's bodyguards to the desert compound.

"You're too quiet, man," Kyle accused his usually talkative sidekick.

"Chill, man," Blackie snapped as he looked in the back storage area to inspect five large blue backpacks full of Fentanyl purple-colored tablets. The purple was an Aguapa product signature with AM, Aguapa Mentaje's initials stamped on each tablet.

Next to the SUV driver, the bodyguard popped one of those tablets without water. Minutes into the drive, he was feeling copasetic. Blackie smiled for the first time, watching the about-to-drool bodyguard.

Kyle shook his head with worry. "We're toast if anyone attacked us right now," he whispered to Blackie, who ignored him and instead polished and nursed a black Uzi on his lap.

"Is that thing loaded?" Kyle asked.

The driver stared at him from the back mirror. "It's useless without bullets, senora."

"Fuck you," Kyle replied, causing everyone to bust out in laughter, except the nearly comatose bodyguard on a Fentanyl high.

Five hundred yards behind, three SUVs followed them, full of El Choco's men.

At the desert compound, Blackie gathered three of the "imprisoned" illegal immigrants in a room where a topographical map of the desert lay on the table.

An Indian, a Bosnian, and a Chinaman, the immigrants watched as Blackie pointed out track locations on the map, explaining the upcoming trip.

The Chinaman flatly stated, "My wife and son are coming with us." Blackie shrugged noncommittally and continued his directives.

Emboldened, the Bosnian said, "My wife is also coming." Blackie eyed him more assertively but continued talking.

Then, the Indian chimed in, "I'm not leaving without my son."

Blackie stopped talking and stared hard at the immigrants. "I will advise against bringing excess baggage, but if you insist, you're responsible, and I will leave you behind in the desert if you slow us down." He looked around for comments, but there were none.

"We leave tonight at dark."

Blackie, Kyle, and the two Aguapa bodyguards set off once it was dark outside, each with a backpack containing mostly water bottles, extra bullet clips for their Uzis, and dried beef jerky. Kyle had no weaponry. He didn't want any despite the insistence by Blackie.

Blackie and the two guards wore night-vision binoculars around their necks.

"You may live to regret your choice or die by it."

"I don't like guns. They make you do strange things by bestowing you a false sense of strength and security."

Blackie chuckled. "Coyotes, don't share whatever you just said."

"No guns. I'll take my chances."

The illegal immigrants all had backpacks loaded with Fentanyl tablet packages, including water and food. The kids and the wives had only small backpacks with water and food.

The terrain was vast and varied, with flood plains, canyons, steep hills, and mesas.

Mesas featuring flat-topped hills bounded from all sides by steep escarpments standing above surrounding plains, much like when a table stands above the floor upon which it rests.

At the top, a mesa consisted of flat-lying soft rocks capped by layers of harder rocks.

The first night was uneventful as the bodyguards, familiar with the route, expertly guarded the crew, except for a few occasions when the kids needed to relieve themselves, which forced a slowdown that peeved Blackie.

"You must control your welp," Blackie yelled at the Indian at first, and then an hour later at the Chinaman.

"The next time they have the urge, I will not stop. Control them eating and drinking all that shit in their mouths."

Meanwhile, the El Choco group, also familiar with the trail, kept its distance but never lost sight of the Blackie team.

As they left the flat flood plains, the trek became more arduous in the canyons, where they had to navigate narrow passages between high rock walls carved over millennia.

The Bosnian scuttled up to Blackie, begging for a breather. Blackie refused.

The El Choco team closed the distance, utilizing the jutted angles of the canyon rocks to hide in crevices that obscured their presence.

Blackie, next to Kyle and behind a guard, all in a single file, commented, "I'm surprised you're keeping up, Negro."

"Don't call me that," Kyle protested as he sipped from the water bottle.

"It means black, not nigger, hombre," Blackie deflected.

"I don't care. I hear something else when you say that," Kyle protested.

"But you call me Blackie all the time," Blackie challenged.

"Your ancestors weren't slaves, were they?" Kyle spat. Blackie ignored the chide.

The second bodyguard brought up the rear.

The third day saw the Blackie team approach the more challenging part of the route: the steep hills.

Blackie halted the troop and announced that everyone should rest up, eat, relieve themselves, and be ready for the climb.

As they ascended, the Indian boy slipped. His father, behind him, couldn't catch him. Kyle dashed like a possessed man, sliding fast down the slope to stop the boy from falling off a cliff.

"Thank you, thank you," the Indian father groveled as they cleaned the boy's lacerations and returned to the trek.

"You're a bleeding heart, Kyle. But I am glad you saved the kid," Blackie lauded.

Kyle cleaned up his scrapes and wounds as they continued.

The El Choco team watched the mishap and had to alter their plans, as they had intended to take the Blackie team as soon as the steep climb began.

The fourth day was at the mesa, where, running out of time, the El Choco team struck.

The assault began when the Indian father accosted Blackie again, saying that his son wanted to take a shit. Blackie didn't understand what the man said. It sounded like "boobdy, boobdy, boobdy," to Blackie, who shook his head for no.

Five minutes later, collective chilling coyote howls dominated the night.

"What the hell was that?" Kyle asked.

"Coyotes," the front bodyguard confirmed, and then continued.

"They're either about to hunt or feeding."

"Are we safe?" Kyle asked.

"As long as you don't break the rank, yes," the bodyguard confirmed.

The Indian father resisted, slowed down with his son, and fell behind the guard, bringing up the rear as the team progressed.

The Indian and his son fell farther and farther back.

Ten minutes later, when they still hadn't returned, the Indian wife began to cry, stopping the whole team. Blackie was afraid of the noise carrying through the night.

Unbeknownst to Blackie and the team, five minutes after the Indian and his son fell behind, two El Choco scouts had snuck behind the Indian man, watching his son stoop, taking a shit, and one of them slit his throat. Simultaneously, the other suffocated the kid.

They dragged the bodies under a brush and ran back to their team, only yards behind.

The coyotes howling Kyle heard were feeding on the dead bodies.

Kyle and the front bodyguard traced back to find the Indian and his son as Blackie tried to console the wailing wife.

In a frenzy, the bodyguard sighted a pack of coyotes a hundred yards from them. He stopped Kyle.

“It's too late, hombre,” he said, confusing Kyle.

“What?”

“I think they’re dead.”

“How do you know that?” Kyle asked.

He thrust his night vision at Kyle, who looked.

“Jesus,” he said as he saw the dreadful feeding frenzy scene.

“We gotta head back,” the guard announced as he snatched the binoculars from Kyle.

To stop the Indian wife from wailing uncontrollably, she was dosed on Fentanyl and led by hand by the Bosnian’s wife.

Kyle, next to Blackie, asked, “What happens now?” Blackie, in surprise, was uninterested. “Nothing. This is the risk.”

“Just like that?”

“Yes, just like that, Kyle.”

Blackie then pointed to a section a thousand yards away, where they sat on the mesa.

“We’re close to the hole.”

“The hole?”

"That's the safest point to cross," Blackie announced.

"This is what we do, Kyle. Millions of dollars are in those backpacks and must get across," Blackie continued.

"That much?" Kyle raised his brows in shock.

"Americans can never get enough of this shit. We wholesale, and Brass's team distributes with crazy markups," Blackie confirmed.

"I'm not sure this is all worth it."

"You shouldn't have stiffed Brass Nacchio on the bank heist job."

"Fuck you," Kyle concluded as they sat resting before the finale.

The last part of the trip was at the mesa separating Tijuana from the crossing point into the United States.

The El Choco team geared up and surrounded the team from four angles as the Blackie team sat on the top-level portion of the mesa, resting before the last thrust.

The rear bodyguard heard the rustle as the El Choco team opted for a frontal assault, rushing from all angles, guns blazing, to massacre the unsuspecting, resting Blackie team.

As the gun battle raged on, Kyle instinctively took off running.

Blackie saw Kyle take off amidst gun muzzle flashes and gave him cover from an El Choco man shooting at him.

Kyle paused briefly, looked back, and saw Blackie, who frantically waved him to keep going with one hand while the other fired at the assailant.

The assailant then directed his full barrage at Blackie, and then three other assailants, having dispatched the Aguapa bodyguards, joined in.

Blackie stood no chance as he went down in a hail of bullets. Perforated with steel slugs and bleeding all over and from the mouth, he snickered, mouthing, "...fucking Negro..."

Sliding fast down the mesa as the shootout went into higher gear, Kyle didn't stop running towards the hole gap.

The farther he ran, the less he heard of the ra-ta-ta-tap of guns shooting. He stumbled, strained his knee, got up, and hobbled until he saw the gap.

Just before he crawled under and collapsed on the other side, he looked back to see smoke and a ball of fire from atop the mesa.

Back at the mesa, the guard and Blackie formed a circle around the immigrants and held off the El Choco team's penetration for a long time, until the immigrants could no longer stand it and began to run, breaking the protective ring. It was just a matter of time before the El Choco team overwhelmed and killed everyone, losing just two of their comrades.

Just as the gunfight ensued, it stopped in eerie silence.

The El Choco team inspected the damage, collected all the bags and guns, and set the bodies ablaze.

Limping badly, Kyle Pearse navigated himself out of the hole and milled amongst people looking for a phone booth, having lost his cell phone.

After an hour, he found a phone booth still functional at a 7-11 store.

He called Billy Pearse, his older brother.

Lying beside his girlfriend, Carmen Soto, Billy looked at the phone as the operator asked a question about accepting a collect call. He showed it to Carmen and was about to hang up.

"It could be an emergency," she said.

"I'll accept," he said.

"Please don't hang up, Billy; I am in a real jam this time."

Billy held the phone away from his ear for a long time, deciding whether to answer. He covered the mouthpiece and spoke to Carmen, who was staring at him.

"Kyle," he said.

"Answer it, for God's sake," she scolded.

"What is it this time, Kyle?"

"I just crossed the border from Tijuana and am about twenty miles from you. I'm sure I'm in trouble from some mean people..." interrupted. "Again?"

"It's serious this time. Some people will come after me and possibly you, but Sylvia..."

Billy snapped upright from the bed. "You dragged her into your shit?"

"You gotta hide me, man."

"Where?" Billy asked.

"Anywhere, bro."

Billy looked at Carmen, who was standing now as well. "He's your brother, Billy!" she said.

The line went silent for a long time before Billy spoke. "Can you get here?"

Kyle, resting on two makeshift crutches, "No. My knee is badly sprained, and I have no money."

Billy thought for a long time as Carmen admonished him into action with one determined expression.

"Wait there. Where are you?"

Chapter 23

Billy drove to the 7-11 and found Kyle cowering behind the orange, green, and red logo store.

"Is that him?" Carmen asked.

Billy squinted at a tattered, tall, good-looking guy limping towards them. "Yes."

"Thank you for coming, Billy. I'm so fucked up...sorry." He looked briefly at Carmen, who marveled at how disheveled Kyle was.

Kyle continued, "Can I borrow your phone? I have to call my wife."

Billy swerved off the road in shock and quickly corrected.

"You're married?" Billy asked with a surprised-laden voice.

"Yes, to Valencia."

Billy passed him his cell phone.

Kyle called using the speaker phone option. "Hi, babe..." he began to say when she cut him off.

"What the hell?" Kyle swore and dialed again.

"...get rid of that fucking phone, mi amore, and call her..." The line went dead again. Kyle caught on, while

Billy and Carmen were just agog as they arrived at Carmen's home.

"What was that all about, Kyle?" Billy asked as he drove him to a doctor he knew in El Cajon, who would not ask questions because of the wound.

Kyle began recovery days later and hopped on real crutches at home with Billy and Carmen.

By now, Kyle had explained his situation with Valencia and all the other current drama in his life.

"Jesus," Billy lamented as he saw the bullet wounds on Kyle's body.

Kyle explained to Billy how the Cartel operated.

"The Cartel business involves bugging everybody's phone and all communication devices of their workers and enemies."

They both walked into the kitchen, where Carmen was cooking.

"Five minutes, boys," she announced.

Billy and Kyle sat in the lounge.

"Where does Sylvia fit into all this mess?" Billy asked.

Kyle explained the Alonzo/Brass connection, then raised concerns about Valencia again.

"I have to call my wife, Billy. She's pregnant and..."

Billy interrupted with an agonized facade. “Do you think her father will harm her?”

“Never. Aguapa adores her, but she could lead him to me… us. That would be bad.”

“So, are you just gonna leave her at his mercy?” Billy asked sternly. Kyle riled up.

“No. I didn’t understand what Valencia meant by calling ‘her’ when we briefly spoke.”

“Then think, damn it,” Billy said as Carmen announced the food was ready.

Within hours of the Aguapa Mentaje’s men massacre at the mesa, a package was left in front of the hacienda home by a biker who took off before security could accost him.

Afraid it was a bomb or some explosives, the security detail carefully opened the package and reared back when three severed human heads, Blackie and the two bodyguards, stared back at them with dead eyes.

Aguapa was not pleased. He called Valencia immediately.

“Your DEA boyfriend led my men to an ambush. I knew…” Valencia hung up on her father, who immediately called back.

“I’m sending my men over to bring you home right now…” Aguapa yelled. Valencia hung up again.

She scrambled to pack her things and busted out of her home, instructing her security to maintain the facade that she was still there.

Valencia headed to the home of her college friend, with whom she had dined at her attempted kidnapping, and who was present at her marriage.

“Hola. I’m on my way. Tell no one I am with you, especially if my father or his men call,” Valencia instructed as she fitted herself and a bag at the back of an Uber.

It was now early morning. Kyle, sleeping on the sofa bed in the lounge, jumped up as Carmen entered the kitchen.

“You scared me,” she said, hand on her heart.

“I know what ‘her’ meant. I gotta make a call,” Kyle told Carmen as Billy entered the lounge.

“Coffee,” he said to no one in particular, but Carmen started filling the coffeemaker with water.

“I know what ‘her’ meant,” Kyle repeated.

“I heard,” Billy confirmed, extending his cell phone to Kyle.

“Is this the new cell phone?” he asked.

"Yeah," Billy confirmed.

Kyle placed the call on speaker as all three eagerly listened. Billy and Carmen were sipping coffee.

"Hi, babe," Kyle said, and Valencia began crying in her friend's tiny apartment.

"How are my babies?" Kyle cooed.

"No time to waste. I need to get out of here before my father finds me."

"Text me the address," Kyle replied, looking dolefully at Billy.

"We only have hours or maybe one day before they find me."

"My brother's got this," Kyle said. Carmen smiled, and Billy was stone-faced.

"Who?" she asked.

"Billy. My big brother."

"The one that..." Valencia began to say before she caught herself.

"Say hello, you're on speakerphone," Kyle announced.

"Hola..." she said and hung up. Kyle sheepishly smiled.

Carmen noted. "She's feisty."

"Oh, you don't know the half of it," Kyle confirmed.

All dressed, Billy announced, "I need to see Father Joe."

"I'm coming with you," Kyle said.

Billy's eyebrows furrowed. "I thought you said bad people were after you?"

"Yeah, but I haven't seen you in like..." he trailed off and looked at Carmen for help.

"You're not walking, are you?" Carmen asked, eyeballing Billy.

Billy grudgingly agreed, and they both left Carmen's home.

"Don't you have your place?" Kyle asked in the car.

"Why did you ask?"

"I only see her stuff, not much of yours."

"You could tell?" Billy asked in surprise.

"Yes."

"I have a condo, but I like living with Carmen," Billy confirmed.

"You don't love her because if you did, you'd be all in and not hedge by keeping your condo," Kyle professed.

Billy snuck a guilty look at Kyle as he parked behind the soup kitchen building.

"Soup kitchen?" Kyle asked.

Billy had had enough. "Any other complaints?"

"Nope, but I am hungry," Kyle smirked as he draped his arm around Billy's shoulder. Billy let it stay as he led them inside.

Father Joe smiled in the empty dining hall, stood up, walked towards the duo, ignored Billy, and opened his arms to a surprised Kyle.

"Welcome, my son. Your brother has never stopped talking about you."

"Billy?" Kyle asked as the embrace lingered.

"As discussed, Father, I'd like to rent your place in Poughkeepsie, New York, to house Kyle and his wife..." Father Joe waved him off.

"Rent? It's empty now, and I wouldn't have it if you hadn't helped," Father Joe retorted. Kyle looked at Billy with admiration.

"Great offer, Father, but I insist on fair market value rental. Isabella will need it."

"Isabella?" Kyle interjected.

“My sister,” Father Joe gently stated, and continued.

“How dangerous are these people we’re talking about? Can’t the police help?”

“No. The Cartel has almost all the law enforcement on their payroll,” Kyle confirmed.

“How soon do you need it?”

“Now, Father. Carmen is talking with his wife as we speak,” Billy offered.

Father Joe turned to Kyle. “You’re married?”

“She’s pregnant, too.”

“Congratulations, my son.”

“When can I pick the keys up? It’s going to be a long drive,” Billy explained.

“Not flying?” Father Joe asked.

Billy shrugged off the question and lied about getting to know Kyle better, but he felt driving was safer.

Father Joe excused himself and soon returned with a large box. “The keys, Billy.”

“Thank you,” Billy said as he got up. Kyle was in tow, leaving the dining hall.

While Billy and Kyle were away, Carmen was on the phone with Valencia to arrange where to meet.

Carmen stood outside the customs area on the San Diego side of the Tijuana-San Diego border crossing. She soon saw a tall, pretty, pregnant lady approaching with only a small purse.

Carmen was expecting someone to carry a traveling valise at least. Their eyes looked, and they simultaneously called out one another's name. They hugged awkwardly.

Carmen began wanting to speak Spanish, but Valencia kept responding in English, so they settled on English.

"Where are your clothes?"

"Do you know any stores around? My clothes don't fit anymore..." Valencia pointed at her belly and continued. "Besides, I didn't want too many explanations at the crossing."

"The baby?" Carmen asked.

"Big girl, always stretching," Valencia proudly explained.

Carmen drove them to the La Jolla mall, closer to her place.

After shopping, Carmen seemed to have bought the whole place, including pants and shirts for Kyle and Billy and an expensive purse for Carmen, which she tried to reject but to no avail.

"It's only money, Carmen. You cannot eat it, no?" Valencia explained that they were struggling with shopping bags as they headed for the parking lot.

The scene was very emotional when Valencia saw her husband and how gaunt he looked. She started crying inconsolably, babbling as she smothered poor Kyle, who was trying to breathe. Billy and Carmen watched, holding hands.

Later that evening, as they dined in the small house, Billy explained the plans and how they would drive to Poughkeepsie, New York. Billy asked if they were safe.

Valencia assured them that her father would not hurt her, but sadly deflected on the safety of others. She thought the East Coast would be the last place her father would look for her.

The next morning, they all left for New York.

"Can I borrow your phone, please?" Kyle asked in the backseat. Valencia curled up to him, snoring.

Carmen passed the cell phone over to Kyle.

"Hello," Kyle said into the speakerphone...

"The number you've called is no longer in service."

"What the hell?" Kyle said in shock, looking at the back of Billy's head.

"That was Sylvia's number. That's never happened before."

Carmen caressed his arm while Valencia, asleep, cozied up even more to Kyle, who wore a disturbed, apprehensive look...

Barely six months pregnant, Valencia suffered a severe stomachache and began to bleed. She screamed, and Carmen rushed to her room.

"You'll be okay," Carmen calmed her down. Her nursing experience kicked into gear while Kyle was shocked and useless to both women.

Ten minutes later, an ambulance emerged from Carmen's cool and collected action.

At the emergency room, Kyle was yelling at the desk nurse, more worried about Valencia's accent than about her condition, when she heard her speak.

"I'm sorry, but I need to see an insurance card," as hospital personnel rushed Valencia into the emergency room.

"They wouldn't let Kyle, who was busy raising a ruckus, in.

"Bastards. You are nothing but money-hungry assholes, " as he paced the passage in front of the theater.

Carmen came out to soothe the restless and the very angry Kyle.

"You're not helping Kyle." She commandingly grabbed his arm and led him away from the desk clerk, who was also losing her patience.

Carmen called Father Joe Fantone.

Half an hour later, a priest in a cassock walked in, spoke with the desk clerk, and handed her the documentation. The priest was the head of the local food kitchen.

Another hour later, Valencia gave birth to a premature girl.

Exhausted, Valencia was drugged into unconsciousness while the newborn was moved into an incubator.

Exhausted, Kyle fell asleep in the waiting room, Carmen next to her as the priest spoke with Carmen.

Later, Carmen finally had time to call Billy to break the news.

"Is she alright?" Bill asked.

"It's touch and go for her, but the preemie is okay for now."

"Thank you, " Billy said.

Billy turned to Sylvia, who was now crying and holding her belly.

Billy put on a brave face. “They’re fine.”

“Are you sure?” Sylvia asked.”

“Yes,” he answered and signaled O’Grady, who came near Sylvia as Billy stepped out for air.

Chapter 24

Sylvia had gotten too big to pole dance and was forced out by Alonzo. Now, always at home, she was unbearable to him each time he was with her.

They had just stopped smoking and sniffing cocaine when Alonzo looked at her and called her a whale. She slowly waddled to the kitchen, grabbed a large knife, and came after him.

"Motherfucker," she said, comically chasing him across the lounge. He slipped, and she sliced him. Outraged, he also shouted, "Motherfucker," and slugged her hard. She fell backward and passed out.

Sylvia Pearse woke up in an emergency room to see heads all around her, in between her legs, doing something. She couldn't move or feel any pain, but she was aware she was in surgery. When she fell, she began to bleed.

Outside, Alonzo and O'Grady loitered. They stayed away from each other until Alonzo couldn't handle it any longer. He walked into O'Grady's face, who slugged him out of anger and frustration.

To the chagrin of emergency hospital personnel, a heavy scuffle ensued, and both grappled on the floor. The desk clerk summoned several hospital security guards who chased both men off the premises.

Outside on either end of the street, each man tended to their wounds.

O'Grady fished for his lighter to light a cigarette. Then his alarm went off because he couldn't find his wallet, which bore his DEA shield.

He panicked and ran inside the hospital, passing a security guard on his way in.

The young, new security guard outside approached Alonzo and thrust a wallet at him.

"That ain't mine," Alonzo said and turned away.

"Aren't you the DEA guy they told me was fighting with another guy inside a while ago? I just came on duty," said the guard.

Alonzo's head spun around when he heard the word "DEA." He approached the man and reached for his wallet.

"No, sir, you said it wasn't yours."

"Can I see inside, though?" Alonzo asked.

"No," said the young security guard as O'Grady came rushing back.

He stopped once he saw a security guard talking to Alonzo, holding his wallet. He ducked back inside as the security guard returned.

O'Grady took back his wallet and high-tailed out of the hospital, knowing he was blown but much more worried about Sylvia, fearing Alonzo would put two and two together.

O'Grady was at the hospital because Sylvia had whispered his number to the nurse during a brief period when she awoke before her admission and then went fully comatose again.

O'Grady, in his car, struggled with what to do next. His feelings for Sylvia won. He called Kyle, but there was no answer. Then he called Billy Pearse.

Billy's phone rang.

"Who's this? And how did you get this number…" O'Grady's authoritative voice kicked in.

"Listen carefully, Billy Pearse. Your sister, Sylvia, is pregnant and in a coma in a hospital in Atlanta. She was my informant, and my cover just got blown…" Billy hung up.

"Prank call," he said to Kyle.

The phone rang again. It was O'Grady. Billy debated whether to answer. Kyle took the phone from him.

"Listen, asshole…"

"Put Billy back on before Sylvia dies from Brass..." O'Grady didn't finish when Kyle panicked and threw the phone at Billy after hearing the name Brass.

Billy picked up the phone. "Who are you? And ..."

O'Grady interrupted, "Listen, idiot, I'm trying to keep Sylvia alive here, and there's maybe only a twenty-four-hour window before she..." Kyle hovered over Billy, listening.

"What's going on?" Billy asked.

"She will be kidnapped, and she will disappear if she's not removed from the hospital quickly."

"How quick is quick?" Billy asked.

"Twenty-four hours at best. I will stall, but can't call this in because I'm already compromised."

"Okay, let me think. Give me your number, and I'll call back within thirty minutes."

"Have you seen her other brother, Kyle?" O'Grady asked.

Billy looked at Kyle, still hovering over him. "Thirty minutes," he said and hung up.

Alonzo returned to the apartment and began to soak, thinking his life was over once Brass Nacchio learned that he'd been harboring an informant for months, privy to their business.

He thought about sneaking up to the hospital and choking the bitch to death, but that asshole DEA agent already knew she was in the hospital.

By now, his nose was red from doing too much coke. He didn't care. He began to dance without music around the lounge, holding an almost-empty bottle of vodka.

In delirium, he began to sing something unintelligible as he collapsed on the sofa.

With finite minutes of his sanity left, he thought about offing himself to save himself from the pain he knew Brass would inflict. He began to laugh deliriously, making several weird killing gestures of throat slitting, hanging, being shot to the head, and drowning until he lay his head on the sofa armrest and passed out.

Predictably, Alonzo woke up with a huge headache and neck pain from sleeping wrong.

He spent the next half hour stretching and coming down from the barbiturate high until Sylvia's treason threw him back into a remorseful demeanor.

"Cocksucker," he said out loud, knowing he'd arrived at a decision.

He would tell Brass about Sylvia snitching, rationalizing that he may be tortured for his gross negligence, but not killed. He grabbed his cell phone.

"I gotta see you now, boss."

Brass made a funny face at Alonzo's request while barbecuing in the backyard.

"Since when do you call before you show up?"

"Serious shit, boss," he explained.

"Get your ass over here, then." Brass hung up and turned to Aguapa Mentaje at the grill, turning chorizos.

"¿Qué pasa?" Aguapa asked.

"Alonzo," Brass confirmed as he opened a new bottle of Pinot Grigio.

After Aguapa Mentaje received the unwanted gory gifts from El Choco, his nemesis, he chapped at the absence of Kyle Pearse's head.

"Pendejo escaped again. Voy a encontrarte, lo prometo," he said out loud as he inspected the maggot-ridden heads.

Two weeks later, he arrived in Atlanta to find the Negro.

"Where is he?" Aguapa launched the verbal assault at his long-time partner even before his bodyguards had brought in his luggage.

"Hello to you, too, amigo." Brass softened the situation.

"Do you know where the Negro you sent to me is or not?" Aguapa insisted, unable to let go.

"No, but we'll find him if you just calm down."

"I cannot calm down, I have three heads sent to me, including your man, Blackie! I liked him," Aguapa confessed.

"So did I, my friend, but we'll find that low life." Brass continued to appease the Mexican Cartel boss, who hadn't yet finished.

Chewing the butt of a fat cigar before he lit it, he went off again. "The Negro also stole my hija, do you know that?"

"We'll find him," Brass continued to calm his angry guest down.

By the end of the second day of his arrival, Aguapa had settled down and calmed enough to start plans on finding Kyle, not only to avenge the death of his men but also the loss of $14 million in product.

Brass was tempted to remind his guest that his rival, El Choco, was responsible, but knew that would incite a new set of angst he didn't want.

And so it was that Alonzo arrived at Brass Nacchio's home and reinvigorated Aguapa's anger when he delivered his news to the two capos who had already left the poolside barbecue, smoking cigars in the lounge.

Alonzo was surprised to see Aguapa and greeted him befittingly. Brass immediately interrupted before Aguapa could be riled up again. "What's this important news?"

Alonzo became coy as he delivered the news. "Sylvia is a snitch for the DEA."

The room went silent; even the bodyguards in the lounge, serving their bosses, froze.

"And you know this how?" Aguapa spoke before Brass could.

Alonzo faced Brass. "She was at the hospital, and a guy…" He told them an abbreviated version of his discovery.

"Where is the agent now?" Brass asked.

"That's the wrong question," Aguapa interrupted and continued. "We need to get this woman and find out where her brother is."

Brass's demeanor appeared calm on the outside. Still, he churned internally, knowing the right move was to find out what the DEA agent knew about their business before planning any personal retribution. But he didn't offer any of that information.

"I agree," he said to the happier Aguapa and looked at Alonzo.

"How long do we have to get her out of there?"

"We have time, boss. She's unconscious."

Once Billy hung up on O'Grady, he called Father Joe with an elaborate plan that even Kyle was stunned by.

"Sylvia is in trouble, and it will take a miracle to get her and all of us out of it, Father."

"Miracle is what the Lord does. How can I help?"

Billy laid out his plans as Kyle listened with rapt attention. Kyle shook his head at some of the elements, forcing Billy to keep moving farther away from him as he explained to the cleric.

Billy called O'Grady back as promised after the call with Father Joe.

"I will fly down to Atlanta today. It's only a few hours, but you must do some heavy lifting before my arrival if you want to help."

“I’m listening,” O’Grady replied, puffing even more vigorously, lurking out of sight at the hospital, wary of Brass Nacchio and his group taking drastic actions.

Billy hung up and instructed Kyle not to breathe a word to the two women.

“Why?”

“There’s enough chaos already; before you ask, you’re not coming.”

“Screw that,” Kyle rejected in a louder voice than Billy wanted.

“Cool it, Kyle. You’d be more of a hindrance. They’re looking for you. Besides, I can’t leave the women alone, right?”

“Valencia can take care of herself; trust me on that,” Kyle offered, arguing about accompanying his elder brother to save their sister.

“What about Carmen?” Billy asked.

Kyle’s demeanor collapsed as he begrudgingly accepted the rationale for him to remain behind in New York.

“You have to call me immediately when you need me. It’s all about Sylvia now, not me, Billy.”

Billy man-hugged his brother as he left for the bedroom to pack for his trip.

O'Grady kicked into action, first calling his boss to pitch the idea of a possible trap for Brass Nacchio that could occur within weeks, but would require extra funds to bait it. He did not mention his compromised situation with an informant or what he'd used the additional taxpayer's money for.

O'Grady figured not to suffer too much if Brass was nabbed. He might even be heralded as a hero, he fantasized.

O'Grady next went into the hospital in disguise to determine if Brass Nacchio's men, especially Alonzo, had posted guards around Sylvia. There were none.

He then snuck into Sylvia's room, who had woken up in a foul mood.

"What the fuck do you want now?" she challenged as she saw him looking at her belly.

He pulled up a chair next to her bed and positioned it so anyone looking in through the glass window on the door wouldn't see him.

He leaned closer; she reared back. "Billy and I plan to get you out of here."

Sylvia jumped up, almost ripping the drips off her arm. "Ouch, that hurts," she said, continuing, "My brother, Billy? How the hell do you know him?"

“That’s not important now, but you must play along when I return to get you out of here.”

“I ain’t going nowhere with you. For all I know, you don’t even know Billy.”

O’Grady was losing time, as he still had other arrangements to make to pull her disappearing act off without alarming the hospital. He got hard with her.

“Listen, you dolt, you think I’d be risking my career to save anyone else but you? Here’s what you’ll do.

“In three hours, unless I return, figure out a way to get yourself out of this room without being noticed and wait at the smoker’s spot.”

She sulked, but she did believe him. “Why didn’t Billy call me?”

“He’s in the air now, on his way here.”

A smile that soon disappeared flashed, and then she began sobbing, surprising O’Grady.

“What in the hell are you crying for?” he asked in complete befuddlement.

“You wouldn’t understand,” she said, wiping off tears.

“Well, stop it,” he said as he rose. “I gotta go. Be ready.” What if Alonzo returns?” she asked with truculence.

“Pick a fight with him to make him leave and stick with the plan.”

“Easy for you to say,” she said, cupping her large belly. “It’s a boy, you know,” she added as his hand reached for the door handle.

He stopped, didn’t turn around, paused for seconds, and left without looking at her.

Chapter 25

Sylvia was antsy as she opened closets to retrieve her stuff. She stared out the window.

At first, Sylvia saw nothing, but then she saw a white van. She didn't think it was threatening, but it still gave her the willies.

All packed up, she went to the bed, fully dressed but with a hospital gown atop, tight at the belly. She laughed at how ridiculous she looked and then covered herself with a linen sheet up to her neck, timing it so the nurses wouldn't make their rounds.

"How are we doing?" The nurse asked.

"Tired," Sylvia faked a yawn and had to shift to cover the IV she had removed from her arm.

The nurse checked the clipboard, looked her over, and left.

Sylvia went to the door, peered through the open cutout glass, and snicked out, using the staircase.

Right then, on the Highway, an hour away from the hospital, Alonzo, on the passenger side of a black van with dark-tinted windows, flipped open a black leather box, took out a filled syringe, pulled off the plastic needle covering, pumped the piston to expel air, replaced the needle covering, and returned the box to his jacket inside pocket—all in seconds.

"Pull over in front of the hospital emergency door," he instructed his partner, driving while two of Aguapa's bodyguards sat in the back.

Aguapa had insisted they accompany Alonzo as they were pining to avenge their "Colegas sin cabeza," as he put it.

"Stay here," he said to Aguapa's men as his driver idled the engine.

He walked briskly inside the hospital to the right floor, not realizing Aguapa's men were behind him until he was at the desk. They stayed yards behind him as he queried the desk clerk.

"Sylvia Pearse's room, please?"

The clerk stared at him funny.

"What's wrong?" Alonzo asked.

"She left."

"What?"

"She left," she repeated, calling the next person in the queue behind Alonzo, who refused to move.

"You must be mistaken," he insisted.

“Sir, please step aside and wait for my supervisor if you wish, but he’ll tell you the same thing.”

“Bullshit,” he bellowed as he rushed off, Aguapa’s men in tow.

“Where is she?” one of them asked as they walked.

“Gone,” Alonzo said as they filed out the front door.

“Where?” the second bodyguard asked.

“How the fuck should I know?” spewed out of Alonzo’s mouth.

“Hijo de puta,” was the reply he got.

It was early evening when O’Grady picked up Billy Pearse in an ambulance at the Hartsfield-Jackson Atlanta International Airport, with lights flashing at the arrivals’ front exit door.

Waiting at the curb, in the driver's seat, O’Grady saw Billy and waved him over, but he turned away, thinking it was in error.

When their eyes met again, O’Grady waved again. Billy ignored him once more. O’Grady then exited the vehicle and walked up to Billy.

“Billy Pearse?”

Billy stayed muted, staring down the man in front of him. Then, he beckoned for an ID. O'Grady showed him one.

"An ambulance?" Billy commented.

"The best disguise possible."

Flying down the Highway, Billy chuckled. "Very clever. I didn't see that coming."

"No sane person stops an ambulance. And this is legit," O'Grady bragged.

"Is she prepped and ready?"

"Yes," O'Grady confirmed as Billy's cell phone rang. It was Kyle.

"Yes, I'm here, but I haven't met Sylvia yet," Billy said before Kyle could utter a word.

"I'm at the hospital. Valencia just had her baby." Kyle confirmed.

"What?" Billy said, alarming O'Grady. Billy waved to calm him down.

"But I thought she was only about six months pregnant?" Billy noted.

"Yes, I think all this excitement pushed the timing. I'm so happy Carmen was here. I forgot you told me she was a nurse, but boy, was she good." Kyle yodeled with excitement, not allowing Billy to get a word in.

"How's Sylvia?" Kyle asked before Billy could respond.

"Valencia agreed to name her Florence... Isn't that great?"

"Yes, yes, I'm so happy and proud..." Billy said as O'Grady pointed at the upcoming turn, which showed the hospital sign.

"I gotta go, Kyle, but I'll talk to you in about thirty minutes or earlier." He hung up before Kyle could protest and turned to O'Grady.

"I just became an uncle... yes, me." Billy gushed.

O'Grady looked at the stoic man he had confronted just minutes ago at the airport, grinning from ear to ear.

"Congratulations..." O'Grady said, then pointed to a figure standing afar in a hospital gown. "That's Sylvia."

The ambulance pulled up in front of Sylvia, who rolled back in surprise.

Billy exited and approached Sylvia, who didn't recognize him at first. It'd been decades since Billy dropped off a nine-year-old Sylvia with Nana Bertha.

"Hello Sylvia," Billy said, approaching her slowly.

Puzzled, Sylvia looked closely, and some recognition dropped.

"Billy?" she called out tentatively.

"Yes, it's me, Sylvia..." He began to say that when O'Grady got out of the vehicle, He rushed Sylvia to the back of the ambulance and firmly pushed Billy inside with her.

"Catch up, but not here," he said as he drove off, heading back to the Highway.

Sylvia sat on the stretcher, not looking at Billy.

"You abandoned me, Billy; I was only nine years old. You abandoned me!" she screamed as she cupped her pregnant belly.

Billy's head hung low, and he remained quiet.

In the cab, O'Grady listened to the drama unfold through a speaker at the back.

Sylvia began to sob quietly at first, then loudly. Billy vacillated between holding her and not, unsure of what to do.

"I'm sorry, Sylvia, I'm so, so sorry," Billy kept repeating through her crying.

Minutes later, Sylvia cried out, looked up, and carefully perused Billy. "You got old," she observed.

"Time does that to you, kid," Billy offered and then continued. "You got pretty, Sylvia, very pretty."

Sylvia slowly leaned forward and hugged her brother, whom she hadn't seen for many years.

They stayed in the embrace for as long as O'Grady drove until Billy remembered something.

"I've got great news," he announced and continued. "Kyle's wife just had a baby, and they named her Flo..."

Sylvia interrupted, breaking the hug, "Kyle is married and has a baby?"

"Yes, they named her Florence," Billy repeated, but Sylvia was too angry to grasp the implication of the baby's name.

"He got married and never told me?" she spewed angrily.

Billy calmed her down. "Be happy for Kyle and Valencia now, Sylvia."

She shot him a nasty look. "Why? Don't I matter?"

"You do, kid, you do. And I'm here now. Be happy for Kyle, please."

Sylvia went quiet, sat back in repose, but remained sulking.

"I'm here now, kid, I'm here," Billy repeated as he pulled out his cell phone and dialed Kyle.

O'Grady's voice came at them from the cab microphone through the back speakers.

"1,300 miles to go, folks, so sit back. We have almost twenty hours of driving."

Sylvia stared at Billy curiously from the cryptic message.

"I'll explain after we talk to Kyle," Billy said as Sylvia, still brooding, sat with arms folded atop her pregnant belly.

Before Billy Pearse left New York after O'Grady's safety alert of Sylvia, Billy, on the phone, had vigorously negotiated with Father Joe Fantone to hide Sylvia at the nunnery where Father Joe's sister, Isabella Fantone, had lived all her life.

"I value you as a friend, confidant, and savior, but Isabella is as fragile as you discovered when you saw her," the papal explained.

"I understand, sir, but I could think of no other place safer than that. Please, Father?"

"Why not bring Sylvia to Poughkeepsie?"

"I would, Father, but all our safety eggs would end up in a single basket," Billy explained.

Father Joe paced his small office in San Diego, and Billy, on the phone in New York, allowed the quiet to settle, praying Father Joe's compassion would outweigh his resistance. The phone crackled.

"I will speak with the Abbess and tell Isabella to expect you. All the best, Billy Pearse," Father Joe acquiesced.

Now, in the ambulance, less than five hundred miles to go, O'Grady announced his need to rest.

"I can drive while you sleep," Billy offered from the passenger seat as Sylvia slept in the back.

"I can't let you do that, Billy: regulations."

"What regulations?" Billy challenged.

"This is now a government vehicle that can only be driven by a government employee," O'Grady explained.

"You don't strike me as a fuddy-duddy rules guy," Billy observed.

"I'm not, believe me, but my career is on the line, and any blemish will scrap my decades of pension/retirement investment," O'Grady espoused as a motel gas station sign came up.

The ambulance took the exit.

All three sat at dinner in the small motel dining hutch.

Sylvia was in front of a plate of pizza slices and tubs of vanilla ice cream, alternating between the two.

Both men ignored her as they chatted.

“Why were you in Atlanta?” Billy asked.

“That’s confidential,” O’Grady said.

“He wanted to nab Alonzo and Brass Nacchio for Fentanyl distribution,” Sylvia blabbered between a mouthful.

“Jesus, keep it down,” O’Grady admonished.

“Do you have what you need on them?” Billy asked.

“He’s got nothing, just used me,” Sylvia stated again.

Exasperated, O’Grady stood up and left the table. “I need a smoke.”

“Take it easy on him,” Billy suggested to Sylvia, who waved over the waiter. “Another scoop, please.”

She then turned to Billy. “We wouldn’t be in this mess if he hadn’t railroaded me into his shit.”

“He’s trying to help now. Cut him some slack.”

Sylvia looked up at Billy. “You got old but are still very handsome. You married, too?”

Billy smiled. “Thank you. No, but Carmen and I are good together.”

O’Grady returned and announced that they had better get going.

“After my ice cream,” Sylvia stated flatly as the waiter approached.

"Okay, but Brass and his team are probably busy figuring out where we are. I'm sure of it. We gotta move." O'Grady sternly walked off towards the exit.

Billy, expressionless, stared at Sylvia, about to take a spoonful of ice cream.

"Okay, okay," she said, dropping the spoon and waddling off her chair as Billy hurried to help her.

They both headed towards the dining hall exit door.

Alonzo and the bodyguards walked into the lounge dolefully. Brass and Aguapa, smoking, stared them down.

Brass walked up to Alonzo's face. "Where is she?"

"I don't know."

"What the fuck do you know?" Brass challenged as one of Aguapa's bodyguards whispered into Aguapa's ear.

Aguapa approached. "She was your girlfriend. Were you in on it with her?"

"Fuck you," Alonzo replied in Aguapa's face. An Aguapa bodyguard moved up, and Aguapa waved him to stay.

In a conciliatory tone, Aguapa turned to Brass and dragged him away from the others to a corner out of earshot. "What do you know of this DEA agent?"

“Not much. The agent is new to this jurisdiction because all the others in the field are on our payroll,” Brass explained.

“What about your head honcho, the DEA guy in DC?”

“He retired,” Brass confirmed, then continued, “Why don’t we go after Kyle?”

“No. Kyle’s probably with Valencia, and we wouldn’t find her if she didn’t want to be found. Plus, Kyle is for later. We need this Sylvia person because we don’t know what she told the DEA guy,” Aguapa explained.

“So, what do you suggest?”

“Money. Throw lots of money and crypto around on the Dark Web.”

“What?” Brass asked in confusion.

“Anonymous greedy people will help us. You’ll see we have the means; the information will surface.”

Aguapa walked off and got on his cell phone as Alonzo scurried to Brass, who walked away from him. Aguapa’s bodyguards snickered at the rejection. Alonzo followed Brass as he left the lounge and headed to the pool area.

Outside, he turned to Alonzo when the sliding door shut behind them.

“We’re fucked because of you. How will you make this right?” Brass inquired.

"I'll do whatever you want."

"Keep that in mind as this shit unfolds." Brass walked back into the lounge, leaving Alonzo outside.

"We'll have something in twenty-four hours," Aguapa announced.

"Like what?" Brass asked.

"I'll let you know!" Aguapa confirmed.

Aguapa Mentaje then sequestered himself in a wing of Brass's mansion with his men.

He put up a million dollars in Cryptocurrency on the dark web, offering rewards for information about the photographs of Blackie, Sylvia, and Agent O'Grady posted there. He debated whether to put up Kyle's picture, but was afraid of dragging his daughter, Valencia, into the search.

His directives encouraged the web to troll, crawl, and dig for surveillance camera footage on highways, motels, malls, small suburbs, and large cities.

Chapter 26

The isolated Abbey of St. Walburga, founded in 1935 from the Abtei St. Walburg, is a Benedictine Roman Catholic monastery located in Virginia Dale, Colorado, led by an Abbess, and boasts devoted nuns in the northern hidden valley of the Rocky Mountains' foothill high plains.

The Abbey's origins are traced back to the early nuns and monks who traveled to the Middle Eastern deserts in search of the Gospel of Christ.

The patroness, St. Walburga (710-779), was a missionary who introduced English Anglo-Saxon Benedictine monasticism to the continent.

Her relics are kept at the Abtei St. Walburg in Eichstätt, Germany, founded in 1035.

O'Grady pulled into the compound of the Abbey, looking around at the vastly unprotected perimeter of the Abbey.

"We'll be sitting ducks here if attacked," he opined.

"No one knows we're here," Billy noted.

"Always prepare for the worst and hope for the best," O'Grady offered as he pulled into the empty parking lot.

"You're very cynical," Billy observed as he exited the ambulance.

"Keeps me alive," O'Grady said as he approached the back to let Sylvia out of the ambulance.

All three walked towards the unremarkable entrance to the Abbey, where two women in black garb, the Abbess and Isabella Fantone, awaited them.

The Abbess, the Abbey's "CEO," waited beside Isabella Fantone as O'Grady, Billy, and Sylvia approached. Isabella rushed to assist the pregnant Sylvia.

"You're about to pop, ain't you?" Isabella stated as she guided Sylvia away from the Abbey front door, surprising both men. The Abbess noticed their concern.

"You will be staying at the guest ranch," she pointed to a single-level abode southeast of the Abbey entrance. She led them behind Isabella and Sylvia.

The visitors didn't realize that Father Joe Fantone had a tough time convincing the Abbess to accommodate them until he proposed a $10,000 donation.

The ranch had five rooms, a kitchen, and two bathrooms. Sylvia headed for the bathroom as Isabella fussed.

So far, Isabella had ignored Billy as if they'd never met. Billy was forced to play along, unsure whether it was deliberate.

Once the nuns left, Sylvia claimed the room nearest the bathroom while O'Grady took the room closest to the door.

"So, what happens now?" Billy asked as they settled in.

"Hopefully, nothing, but I must prepare for the worst."

"How so?" Billy asked.

"I need to call a Poindexter to the party."

"Who?"

"A wannabe 'gangster-nabber,' I know." O'Grady air-quoted, confusing Billy, who walked away as O'Grady dialed on his cell phone and headed outside the ranch.

"Maverick, you in DC?"

"No. Oregon."

"What for?"

"What do you want, O'Grady?"

"You wanna nail a Fentanyl distributor?"

"Yes, if named Aguapa Mentaje."

Maverick was in a Humvee, flying down an Oregon highway, driving. He replied with disinterest.

O'Grady infused seriousness into his voice.

"You're in luck. I have a credible witness sequestered away against Brass Nacchio, but I'm worried the Cartel might find us. I need your help."

"Right now, anyone not named Mentaje is outside my radar. Call your boss," Maverick quipped.

"If we nail Brass, he will sell out Aguapa, you know that," O'Grady proposed.

"True, but that's a long road. I need to catch the Mexican drug dealer red-handed."

O'Grady resorted to guilt. "Just so you know, my witness is pregnant, and I also have her brother here; her other brother is Aguapa Mentaje's in-law."

Maverick slammed on the brakes, swerving like a crazy man over the empty highway.

He parked on the side of the road. "In-law?"

"Yup."

"You wouldn't be..." Maverick's voice trailed off.

"Scout's honor," O'Grady replied.

The line went quiet. O'Grady allowed Maverick to ponder, knowing the longer the pause, the better his chances of getting help.

"What do you need, O'Grady? And don't fuck me on this."

"A squad, at least. Heavily armed."

"You know what a squad is. And the cost implications?" Maverick said.

"Yes. I'd rather it be more than less. You know these Cartel rats don't play."

"When and where?"

"Pronto, my friend. I just texted you the location."

"Colorado? An Abbey?"

"Hiding from the Cartel is all-consuming and has to be crafty. We're waiting." O'Grady hung up.

A squad consists of two teams, each carrying four to ten combatants. The duties are twofold: the base-of-fire element and the maneuverer of the element.

Aguapa Mentaje was deluged with responses to his dark web requests.

They found likely suspects in Poughkeepsie, New York, but the dotards he sent went to Poughkeepsie, Arkansas, allowing Kyle and Valencia to duck a deadly bullet.

Three other leads came from Massachusetts, Boston in particular, where multiple O'Gradys were found, none of which fit what Aguapa needed, including a clip when Blackie was seen and shot at running from a gas station food mart into a car driven by a getaway man that looked like Kyle Pearse.

O'Grady was also seen with a pregnant woman and another man in Colorado. He dispatched a scout who returned with the news of an Abbey hideout.

Aguapa Mentaje and Brass Nacchio's teams geared up for an assault at a Colorado Abbey.

The Aguapa-Brass team arrived in Colorado late at night and assembled at a motel for the final plans.

"What do we do with the nuns?"

"Nothing," Aguapa snapped at Brass, whose nerves had become jangled traveling those miles.

"Take it easy, man, what the fuck," Brass snapped back, fed up with the chatty Mexican.

"Lo siento, mi amigo," he said and continued. "I don't expect the nuns to resist. They're conditioned to be pacifists, plus, what can they do?"

"What if they do?" Brass insisted.

Aguapa shrugged. "Then, we do what we do."

Two of Aguapa's men looked at each other and made a sign of the cross when their bosses were not looking.

"Positioning?" Alonzo asked.

Brass traced the map on the table. "The place is isolated. There's no gate, so they'd see us coming. We position four ways," he pointed, "North, south, east, and west. Aguapa and I will remain in the car farther off the Abbey, watching in case of escapes.

"What happens inside?" Aguapa asked.

"We retrieve the girl and the agent."

"What if they resist?" Aguapa goaded.

Brass stared hard at his long-time partner. "They wouldn't."

"They die if they resist," Aguapa stated, signaling for a drink from the small refrigerator.

He lit a cigar, drank from the bottle, and retreated to the area of the room with the TV.

Brass continued with the plans. "I don't expect any trouble, but if there is, you all know what to do." He looked around to see nods. He packed up the map and joined Aguapa in smoking.

Alonzo and his man left Aguapa's motel room.

Outside, Alonzo turned to his man. "I have a bad feeling about this. It's an Abbey with women, holy women. And I care about Sylvia."

Alonzo's man shot him a quizzical look. "The same Sylvia?"

"Yes. What's so strange about me having a feeling?" Alonzo fezzed up.

"That's a new one," His man replied.

"Watch your mouth, asshole," Alonzo turned hard.

"I'm just saying," the man backpedaled.

"It's a sin, man," Alonzo insisted.

Alonzo's man suppressed a burgeoning laughter as he lit a cigarette. "We sell dope, we sell women, we kill, and now you're a Christian?"

"Fuck you," Alonzo said as he bummed a cigarette.

"We're all going to hell," Alonzo concluded as they walked towards their motel rooms.

Aguapa Mentaje and Brass Nacchio sat in the back of a black sedan, Alonzo driving.

They trailed behind a four-SUV armada, two goons inside each vehicle, as they approached the Abbey in the early evening; it was already dark.

Three SUVs broke off north, east, and west of the Abbey. The fourth parked in front of the Abbey door while the sedan stayed back, 100 yards away, watching. Binoculars hung down the Cartel boss's neck.

Four goons gathered at the door, one from the SUVs, leaving one in each vehicle for security, ready to flee if necessary. With guns drawn, the goons invaded the Abbey.

They searched room to room, finding no one until they reached the chapel, where all the nuns were praying.

One of the goons discharged his weapon in the air, causing a strange, quiet commotion.

Scared, all nuns flinched from their prayer position, nary a sound. The goons looked at each other, wondering what was happening with noiseless response.

The Abbess approached the assailants, making a silent gesture with her hand. The nuns were all observing a vow of silence.

"Fuck this shit," a goon said as he rushed between the nuns, scattering them and segregating them into sections. The other three goons followed his example, herding the nuns into the room's four corners.

The Abbess stepped forward into the face of the lead goon, who asked, "Where are your visitors?"

She made a sign of the vow of silence. The goon made as if to pistol-whip her, but didn't.

"Are there other people in here?" he asked again. She shook her head for no.

A mile away from the Abbey, Maverick McNealy, in a Humvee, on the passenger side, on the radio, gave instructions to two other Humvees behind him as they approached the dirt road leading to the Abbey.

"Lights out, muzzle suppressors on, sniper in position. The base of element combatants, Humvee One, invades, while Humvee Two stays back to maneuver incidentals. Let's go, people."

The two Humvees zoomed past Maverick's vehicle, which coasted slowly behind.

Maverick yelled "stop" into the radio when he saw a sedan moving southeast of the Abbey through his night vision binoculars. Then he widened his gaze to see the Cartel SUVs.

Maverick had seen Alonzo driving the sedan towards the ranch when Aguapa said he thought he had seen some movement there.

“We have hostilities all over, gentlemen. You know what to do,” Maverick announced and then cut the chatter.

The first Humvee approached the Abbey, lights off, and saw the SUV.

A sniper settled on the roof, weapon pointed at the Abbey front door, while the other Humvee took a wide arc encircling the Abbey. It stopped when he saw an SUV. He got on the radio.

“SUV west, suspect another one east and possibly north.”

“Mobile attack commences, pronto. Over and out,” Maverick commanded.

All the men in the Humvees, in dark fatigue and heavily armed, eased out of the vehicles and advanced to invade the Abbey perimeters.

Meanwhile, inside the Abbey, a goon went wild and started smashing all the items in the temple. Some of the nuns began to sob quietly.

The goon who made the sign of the cross rushed to his partner and calmed him down. Isabella, watching, ran up to confront the “Christian” crook.

She faced him, moved the muzzle of his weapon in his hand to her heart as she began to murmur at first until her voice bellowed with oratory vehemence in the assailant's face...

"God hath spoken in his holiness; I will rejoice, divide Shechem, and mete out the valley of Succoth.

"Gilead is mine, and Manasseh is mine; Ephraim is also my head's strength; Judah is my lawgiver.

"Moab is my washpot; over Edom will I cast out my shoe; Philistia, triumph thou because of me.

"Who will bring me into the strong city? Who will lead me into Edom?

" Wilt not thou, O God, which hadst cast us off? and thou, O God, which didst not go out with our armies?

"Give us help from trouble, for vain is the help of man.

"Through God, we shall do valiantly, for he shall tread down our enemies..."

Isabella collapsed in a faint. The goon dropped the gun and fled towards the Abbey's front exit door.

As soon as he opened the door and lurched outside, a high-caliber bullet from a sniper perforated his temple with a deadly, plopping sound.

The combatants on the perimeter silently took out the three SUV drivers, slitting their throats.

"North secured," "West secured," East secured," crackled on the radio.

“Bravo, now the frontal assault, gentlemen,” Maverick commanded.

Chapter 27

The sedan arrived before the ranch as O'Grady, Billy, and Sylvia ate dinner.

They heard the sedan's engine, so O'Grady went to the door to look.

He opened the door and was pushed back inside by Alonzo with a gun.

"Hello, Agent DEA," Alonzo said as Billy and Sylvia rushed out to the lounge from the dining room.

Aguapa and Brass advanced towards them, gun-pointing. "Is she the snitch?" Aguapa asked.

"Yeah," Alonzo answered without looking, his gaze on the DEA agent.

All three crooks, now wielding guns, shooed Billy, O'Grady, and Sylvia to sit on their hands on the sofa, all snuggled up on the two-seater.

Aguapa pulled up a chair in front of them.

"You cost me two good men and $14 million in products," he said to no one.

"And Blackie," Brass interjected and then stared at Sylvia. "What did you tell DEA?"

“Nothing,” O’Grady interrupted. Alonzo moved fast to pistol-whip the agent.

“Asshole,” Alonzo added as O’Grady bled.

Outside, Maverick exited the Humvee with two commandos and carefully approached the ranch.

A commando, using a periscope, looked through the window to see the Cartel men holding hostages.

With hand signals, Maverick directed the two commandos to circle the ranch in case of a breach. They soon returned with a negative response.

Maverick then decided on a frontal assault.

With hand signals, he directed his men to launch teargas grenades through the windows. Seconds later, with face masks, they broke down the front door.

Pandemonium ensued in the lounge as the canisters exploded.

Coughing, sneezing, and teary-eyed, O’Grady rushed to Alonzo. Billy pulled Sylvia to the ground and tried to cover her with his body without crushing her belly as they coughed from the teargas.

Aguapa, coughing and wiping his eyes, began shooting wildly while Brass also ran farther into the house, coughing.

The commandos overpowered Alonzo, who was grappling on the floor with O'Grady.

Maverick, pointing his gun at Aguapa, pushed him towards the door and forced him to open it to dissipate the teargas effect.

Aguapa went for Maverick's gun. Three rapid shots rang out. Aguapa Mentaje died instantly.

The two commandos carefully tracked Brass, who was hidden in the bathroom.

"You have two seconds to surrender..." Brass responded with rapid shots through the door. The commandos obliterated the door and Brass Nacchio behind it. He slumped dead on the toilet bowl.

In the lounge, Billy lifted Sylvia, unharmed, not realizing he'd been shot in the arm until Sylvia screamed.

"You've been shot!" she said.

"It's nothing," he replied while wincing.

"Hostiles dead, over," Maverick announced on the radio, standing next to O'Grady, holding Alonzo's gun to Alonzo's head.

"Acknowledged, over and out," a commando answered from behind the Abbey.

The commandos outside gathered behind the Abbey and organized an assault on the church, climbing through the windows.

Inside, they confronted a hostage situation at the chapel.

The lead commando broadcast through a megaphone, "All your people outside are dead. You can wait this out and die, or take your chances and not die. Your choice."

The hostage standoff lasted for thirty minutes until the goons decided to lay down their arms.

The Abbess attended to Isabella, who had woken up and didn't remember her outburst.

An hour later, the secluded Abbey was overrun with flashing lights from police vehicles, ambulances, and reporter vans.

Soon, Maverick and his men left with their prisoners.

O'Grady, Billy, and Sylvia followed behind in their ambulance.

Several tow trucks were busy hoisting the Cartel SUVs as reporters quizzed the Abbess and Isabella.

Billy called Kyle from a motel near Denver International Airport.

"It's all over, kid. Sylvia and I can't get a flight out for two days, and I have bad news for Valencia."

"What?"

"Her father died struggling to get an agent's gun," Billy announced.

"Oh shit," Kyle said as he walked outside to continue the call. He had been beside Valencia and the baby in the lounge when he picked up the call.

Outside, Kyle asked. "How do I tell her?"

"I will talk with Carmen when I'm done with you to help break the bad news to her. But it must be done as soon as possible, preferably today."

"I understand," Kyle agreed.

"Before I let you go, I need you to organize a homecoming, something for Sylvia..."

Kyle interrupted, "How's she doing?"

"Surprisingly well," Billy confirmed.

The line went silent for a few seconds, then, "How do I organize a party for Sylvia while informing Valencia she had just lost her father?"

"I don't know, Kyle, but it must cross her mind often in the business she grew up in."

"Still," Kyle challenged.

"Carmen will help."

"What happened out there?" Kyle asked.

"I will fill you in on the details, but you must handle the Valencia talk now, kid."

"Okay." Kyle hung up.

Billy called Carmen.

After Billy's call, Carmen took Valencia for a walk while Kyle looked after the baby.

They were just outside the front door when Valencia turned to face Carmen. "He's dead, isn't he?"

Carmen nodded and hugged Valencia, who stepped back, sobbing with her head in her hands. "The bastard," she said, now crying loudly.

Kyle was at the window holding the baby, unsure what to do.

Valencia walked back inside, grabbed the baby from Kyle, and stepped outside again, rapidly walking down the street. Kyle wanted to follow, but Carmen held him back. "Let her grieve the way she knows how."

Kyle and Carmen followed behind her at a distance to ensure her safety.

Half a mile later, she was sitting on a park bench, rocking her sleeping baby back and forth.

Kyle and Carmen slowly approached her.

She looked up. "You wanna hold your child?" she asked, gently handing the baby to Kyle. She then stood up and hugged Carmen tightly.

Minutes later, she let go and headed back home. "Vamos," she said.

The homecoming was a blast and a pleasant surprise for Sylvia, who couldn't stop crying when she held Florence, Kyle's daughter and Sylvia's niece.

Hours into the soiree, Sylvia's water broke, and she was rushed to the hospital.

By the following morning, she'd given birth to a baby boy.

Kyle stood beside Valencia, who was holding Florence; Billy held Carmen's hand, and they all surrounded Sylvia on the bed, where she was resting with the baby on her chest.

She looked up at Billy. "Do you want to hold him?"

"I'd like nothing better," he said.

"What's his name?" Carmen asked Sylvia.

Sylvia first looked at Kyle and then settled on Billy as she announced her son's name.

"Jordan."

END

About the Author's Stories

Yomi Akinode's novels explore the fragile bonds between people, the weight of difficult choices, and the emotional consequences that follow. Each story stands alone but shares a common thread: lives changed by secrets, sacrifice, and the struggle to live with the past.

Please be kind. Leave a pleasant REVIEW if you enjoyed the book.

www.ingramcontent.com/pod-product-compliance
Lightning Source LLC
La Vergne TN
LVHW020659110826
845149LV00012B/2051